NATHAN WRIGHT
[9]

The
Great Rescue
Operation

THE
Great Rescue Operation
Operation

Jean Van Leeuwen

Illustrated by Margot Apple

A YEARLING BOOK

Published by
Dell Publishing Co., Inc.
1 Dag Hammarskjold Plaza
New York, New York 10017

For Bruce,
my *right-hand man*

Yearling·® TM 913705, Dell Publishing Co., Inc.

ISBN: 0-440-43124-7

Reprinted by arrangement with Dial Books for Young Readers,
a division of E. P. Dutton, Inc.

Printed in the United States of America
February 1985

10 9 8 7 6 5 4 3 2

CW

Contents

The
Great Rescue
Operation

1

I Wake Up
the Toy Department

"What would you like to do, Fats?" asks Raymond.

"I don't know, Raymond," says Fats. "What would you like to do?"

It is after lunch. The three of us are sitting around the kitchen table. Our stomachs are pleasantly full of hot pastrami on rye with an order of cole slaw on the side from the delicatessen upstairs. It is our minds that are empty. The days of winter are long and boring in Macy's toy department, where we live.

"How about a game?" suggests Raymond. Ever since he finished reading the entire sixteen-volume set of the *Encyclopedia Britannica,* he has devoted himself to mastering every game in the toy department.

"Okay," agrees Fats.

"Chess?" Raymond proposes eagerly. It is his favorite because it requires so much thinking. Raymond is a great thinker.

"Chess is too hard," Fats objects. "Candyland?" It is his favorite because he loves to look at all that food. Food is his reason for living.

"Too sweet," says Raymond. "Besides, we played that yesterday."

They start arguing about Scrabble and Pick Up Sticks and Monopoly and tiddledywinks. I stop listening. The only thing more boring than playing games is listening to an argument about which game to play. I have better things to think about. Like what to do to bring some excitement back into our lives. For many weeks it has been this way. Ever since Christmas. No more Santa Claus and throngs of children lined up to see him and shoppers loaded down with packages and that dumb song about the reindeer with the nose problem playing over and over on the loudspeaker. The toy department is quiet. Too quiet. Business must be way off. The salespeople sit around and read newspapers and talk to each other about the pain in their left elbow. They don't even notice that Raymond has borrowed their best chess set as a model for the mouse-size set he is carving for himself. Or that Fats has taken to having his afternoon nap in the plush velvet interior of the Dolly-Deluxe model doll carriage. It is like the whole toy department has gone into hibernation for the winter. It is terrible.

"Your turn, Marvin," says Fats.

"What?" I ask, coming to.

"Your turn to pick a card from me," Fats repeats. "Hurry up." He reaches for a tortilla chip from the bag on the table.

I don't even know what game I am playing, but I pick a card.

Fats starts to snicker. The stomach for which he was named bobs violently up and down, nearly upsetting the table. "You got the Old Maid!" He cackles happily.

The Old Maid. This is how low I have sunk. Me, Merciless Marvin the Magnificent, master criminal, master detective, and all-around tough guy. Me, a mouse of the streets, used to danger and darting around, reduced to playing Old Maid. Little did I suspect when I moved into Macy's for the winter that it would come to this.

"Mix up your cards, Marvin," urges Fats. "Now Raymond has to pick."

I mix up my cards. As I do, I become aware of a strange sensation in my toes. A kind of itchiness and twitchiness. I have felt this before. It is an itch for action.

Raymond picks a card. When he sees which one it is, his whiskers quiver and his ears turn pink.

"You got it!" cries Fats. "I can tell. You got the Old Maid!" He leaps up and goes into the strange little dance he always does when he's excited about something, usually cheese. Or his latest favorite, pickles. In his fit of hysterical glee he finally does upset the table. Cards and tortilla chips and fat mice go flying.

That does it. I can't take it anymore.

"You can have your Fireman Freddy and Nurse Nancy," I announce, throwing down my cards. "I'm leaving."

6

They both blink at me.

"Leaving?" repeats Raymond, looking alarmed. "Forever?"

"Can't you finish the game first?" puts in Fats. "It's no fun with just two."

"Not forever," I snap impatiently. "Just for a breath of air. A look around. Something."

Raymond consults his pocket watch. "But, Marvin," he protests. "It's only two fifteen. It's still daytime. You know it's dangerous to go out in the daytime."

"Dangerous, shmangerous!" I snort. "It's not dangerous enough, that's the problem."

With that, I head for the front door.

"Marvin!" they both call out in unison.

I pause next to the door.

"If you happen to see a pickle," says Fats, a silly smile on his face at the thought, "would you bring it back?"

I nod.

"And be careful," pleads Raymond.

"What fun is that?" I reply.

And I open the door.

I haven't lost all caution. First I survey the situation from the doorway. Living in a dollhouse tucked away on a high shelf has its advantages. From here I can see almost all of the toy department. What I see is what I expected. There are maybe two customers in the whole place, browsing quietly among the baby toys. Aside from them, there is no activity. The salespeople are sitting behind their counters, reading newspapers or writing letters or just looking bored. The whole scene reminds me of a line from a book Raymond read to us at Christmas: "Not a creature was stirring, not even a mouse."

One of us is starting to stir now. My next move is to check my listening post. One shelf down, where the doll furniture is kept, I have established the perfect spot for finding out what is going on. It is the bottom bunk of a double-decker doll bed. Concealed here, I am able to eavesdrop on the conversations of two salesclerks who talk a lot: Mrs. O'Grady, who takes care of the doll counter, and Mrs. Feldman, who sells stuffed animals.

Slipping swiftly into position, I listen. I can't believe it. These two ladies, who usually talk all day long, aren't saying a word. I lean over the edge of the shelf to make sure they are still there. They are. Mrs. O'Grady is sitting on a stool, knitting something long and striped, while Mrs. Feldman, a pencil in her hand, studies a page covered with little empty white boxes.

Minutes go by, and still nobody says anything. Mrs. O'Grady yawns. I am beginning to feel a little sleepy myself, when at last Mrs. Feldman speaks.

"Rose," she says, "can you think of a river in Tibet with seven letters?"

Crossword puzzles! I thought Old Maid was a yawn, but sitting around writing words in little boxes is ridiculous. What has the toy department come to, anyway?

It is at that low moment that I have my idea. Just having an idea after all these weeks of doing nothing is an exciting experience, one that sets my toes to tapping, my tail to tingling. And after considering it for a moment, I have to admit it is one of my most brilliant ideas yet. While they are all busy with their boring games and boring puzzles, I am going to play a little game of my own. It is called "Wake Up the Toy Department."

I don't hesitate. I go right into action. For openers,

9

I decide to test how fast asleep these two sales-clerks really are. Boldly I step out from the cover of my listening post. In broad daylight, without even bothering with a disguise, I climb down from the furniture shelf to the doll shelf, to the next doll shelf, and then down to the floor. Mrs. O'Grady and Mrs. Feldman are so busy doing nothing that they don't notice a thing. So I do something even more daring. I drop into Mrs. O'Grady's knitting basket to see if she happens to have any snacks stashed away in there. Nothing: no food and no reaction either. These ladies are out like a light.

So I decide to try something else. Over in the corner there is a bunch of play equipment for little kids: a slide, swings, metal rings, and climbing bars. For weeks now, after the store is closed and no one is around, I have been using this as my personal gym. Here I practice acrobatic stunts, the kind of routine I've seen circus performers do on TV. I've gotten pretty good, maybe even good enough to join the circus myself. And now is my chance to perform in front of a live audience.

Climbing to the top of the slide, I take a quick look around. On second thought I wouldn't exactly say I have a live audience. The salesman nearest to me, at the games and puzzles counter, has his eyes closed, his chin resting heavily on his hands. I'm not quite sure if he is asleep or if maybe he is a statue. Then there is the saleslady at the art counter. She is so busy writing letters that she probably wouldn't notice if the store was on fire. This is the audience I have to wake up. I can see it isn't going to be easy.

To warm up I take a fast ride on the slide, landing neatly on my feet at the bottom. I look around to see if anyone noticed. Games and Puzzles hasn't moved a muscle. Neither has Art. I climb up again. This time I try something a little trickier—my backward, headfirst slide. No response. After a few of these I move over to the climbing bars to perform an aerial routine I've been working on: headstands, handstands, backflips, hanging upside down by my tail—all of it five feet off the ground with no net. I'm really warmed up now. It's a dazzling performance, if I do say so myself. And then I go to the metal rings for the climax of my act—the flying trapeze. Swinging far out into space, I execute a double backward somersault, catching myself by the heels at the last possible second. When I climb back on the bar, I hear the wild clapping of the circus audience, and I take a deep bow. Then I realize it's not wild clapping I hear coming from the games and puzzles counter. It is wild snoring.

Well, at least I know he is not a statue. I look around for a new toy to play with. The electric train, my top favorite, was put away right after Christmas, but on the table where it used to be is an electric racing car set. I've always liked traveling at high speeds. I jump into a yellow sports car and whip around the track, hanging on for dear life as I take the curves. Three times around, and I'm getting a little dizzy. Also, it's not so much fun when there's no one to race. So I jump out. Glancing over at the games and puzzles counter, I see that I have yet to impress him. He is still snoring.

What can I do to get this guy's attention? Suddenly it comes to me. Noise—that's what I need. And my eye falls on just the place to provide it. The music department. Raymond and Fats and I have enjoyed many a midnight concert here, Raymond on xylophone, Fats on triangle, and me on drums. But there is one instrument I've never tried: the electric organ. That ought to be good and loud.

I leap up on the keyboard. My rendition of "Rudolph the Red-Nosed Reindeer" (the only song I know by heart) is a little shaky at first. Playing the organ is harder than the xylophone or drums. I have to use my feet. But soon I get the hang of jumping from key to key, and my "Rudolph" starts to resemble the tune we used to hear hour after nerve-racking hour during those busy days before Christmas.

All the time I'm doing my musical dance, I'm looking over my shoulder. This time I'm positive I'm going to wake the place up. Sure enough, I hear someone grumble, "What is that *dreadful* noise?" And at the games and puzzles counter I see the salesman's chin fall off his hand and his eyes flutter open.

I get ready. As soon as they make a move toward me, I plan to do a fast disappearing act.

But no one is moving toward me. The grumbling stops. And as I watch in dismay, the games and puzzles salesman rearranges himself in a more comfortable position. Little snores once more fill the air.

This is terrible. It's a disgrace. A brass band could march through Macy's, and no one would notice. A lion could stroll through, an elephant—an entire circus.

I look up, imagining acrobats flying through the air. As I do, I see something I never saw before. There is a thin wire running across from the music department to the art counter. It must be left over from the Christmas decorations. Yes, I seem to remember a banner hanging there back in December. But as I look at it, I don't see a wire for hanging Christmas decorations. I see a tightrope.

I've always wanted to try a little tightrope walking. It's the most daring act in the circus. There you are at the top of the tent, your whole body balanced on a single thread, with one wrong step leading to instant disaster. It requires nerves of steel, which I happen to have. I can't wait to try it.

Using some shelves as a ladder, I climb to the spot where the wire is hooked to the wall. I stand there a moment, testing the wire with one foot while still holding on to the wall. This is going to be a cinch. "And now, in Ring Number One," I can hear the ringmaster announce, "demonstrating his magic on the high wire, it's Merciless Marvin the Magnificent!"

I glance down to acknowledge the crowd. This is a mistake. For suddenly I notice that the electric organ, the drums, the cymbals, all seem like doll furniture, I'm so high up. The bald head of the sleeping salesman looks like a miniature egg. And the floor appears miles away and very hard.

I swallow. I take a deep breath. I force my eyes to look up. The show must go on. And I, Merciless Marvin, can do it. I step out on the wire.

It sways. I put my arm out like the circus performers do on TV, and don't move a muscle. The wire steadies. I take another step forward. This really is like balancing on a thread. A very slippery thread. And it's harder for a mouse than a human. I'm not quite sure where to put my tail.

But I inch forward. Another step, and another. I am starting to enjoy myself. I've got it, I think. I am a tightrope walker. The star of the Big Top.

And now for my greatest trick. "Merciless Marvin the Magnificent will now perform a death-defying feat of daring—a headstand on the high wire, with-

15

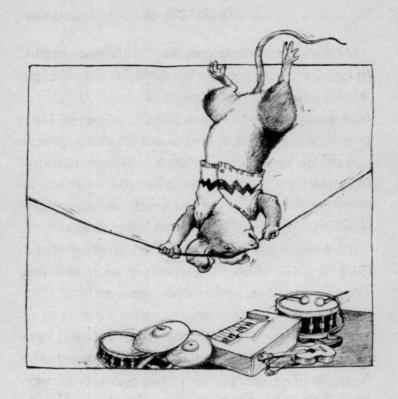

out a net!" announces the ringmaster. The crowd gasps in fear and anticipation.

I grip the wire with my paws. Carefully I lower my head until it rests on the wire. Then, very slowly, I raise my hind legs into the air.

For one glorious moment I perch there, a mighty miniature marvel, balanced on his brain.

And then something goes wrong. The wire begins to sway. Faster and faster it swings, as if in a high wind. I put my arms out to steady it as before, but now my tail is out of balance. I'm falling over. Desperately I try to grab the wire, but it is too slippery.

I plunge to the ground. My last thought is, Why did I insist on performing without a net? But it is too late for regrets. It is too late for everything. I close my eyes as the floor rushes up to meet me.

Clang! It's not the floor that meets me, but the cymbals. *Crash!* Now it's the bass drum. And then, *Ta-ta-ta-tum!* The organ. And then, nothing. The world turns black.

I open my eyes. I am lying on the organ keyboard, which is still playing the same awful chord. Miraculously I seem to be in one piece. But every part of me aches. I feel like I've just gone through all the cycles of a washing machine, including being wrung out and spun dry.

I sit up, shaking my head to stop it from spinning. And then I notice it isn't just me that is spinning. The whole toy department seems to be in motion. People are running and shouting. Some are running toward me: "Don't worry. I'll take care of this!" and some away: "Help! Call the exterminator!" And I realize that I've done it at last. I've woken up the toy department.

A smile steals across my face, despite the fact that the games and puzzles salesman is now wide-awake and bearing down on me with a broom. Making an instant recovery, I scamper along the keyboard, creating new music as I run, then leap to the floor. Someone throws a shoe at me, but I dodge it easily. Then I am off and running, with about six sales-clerks chasing after me.

This is the life I love, darting here, dodging there, always just one step ahead of danger. I lead them on a good chase, out of the toy department, once around the TV sets, then up and over and around and behind washers and dryers, refrigerators and microwave ovens. I make sure I take them far from the dollhouse, where right now Fats and Raymond are having their afternoon naps.

At last I have them totally confused. While they are down on their hands and knees peering into dishwashers and arguing about which freezer to move, I slip over to the luggage department.

Quietly I climb to the top of a pyramid of suitcases. Finding one with its zipper ajar, I crawl inside and curl up in its cozy quilted lining to wait for all of them to go home.

2

I Make
a Startling Discovery

In the dark of night, while the store is sleeping (except for the cop who patrols Macy's, and he is patrolling another floor), I make my way back home. Just to be on the safe side I slip in the back door.

I know my gang will be worried about me, so I'm a little surprised to find only Raymond sitting at the kitchen table, nervously twirling his whiskers and looking like he's lost his last chess piece. Fats hasn't even waited up to see if I brought him a pickle.

When Raymond sees me, he jumps out of his chair. "Oh, Marvin, thank goodness you're back! I've been so worried."

"Worried?" I scoff. "About me? Don't you know by now that Merciless Marvin the Magnificent can take care of himself?"

Raymond starts to reply, but I cut in. "You won't believe the good time I've had. I didn't just wake up those dreamers in the toy department. I turned the place upside down. It was beautiful."

"I heard a lot of noise out there," says Raymond. He still has a worried look, even though I'm standing right next to him. "But, Marvin, something else happened."

"Later, later." I wave my arm impatiently. "First I want to tell you how I single-handedly outwitted an army of salesclerks, all of them out to do me in. And some of them were armed."

"But——" says Raymond again.

"No 'buts' about it. Sit down, Raymond, old boy," I urge, shoving him into a chair. "You're going to love this story."

I settle myself comfortably, my feet on the table, the bag of tortilla chips resting on my stomach. I nibble on them as I recite the heroic tale of my amazing acrobatics on the play equipment, my electrifying entertainment on the organ, my daring deeds on the high wire, and finally my hair-raising chase through not just the toy department but the entire fifth floor of Macy's.

Strangely, throughout my story, Raymond says nothing. He just sits there looking worried.

"One of the salesmen threw a shoe at me," I say to give him something to worry about. "Just missed my right ear."

Raymond nods absentmindedly.

"And I heard them say they were going to call the exterminator."

This reaches him.

"Did you say 'The Exterminator'?" He says it as if just the word could do us in. We have had our moments with exterminators. In the movie theater where we used to live, we had emergency evacuations about once a month. Once we almost didn't make it. The exterminator came in the front door of Raymond's hole just as we were slipping out the back. The fumes were terrible. We barely escaped with our lives. Raymond, who likes to save things, lost all the junk he'd spent months scavenging from under the seats, including the world's largest collection of used bubble gum. He's never quite gotten over it.

"It's okay," I reassure him. "They'll never look for us here. I made sure of that."

But Raymond looks more worried than ever. He's slumped in his chair like a limp noodle.

This is starting to get on my nerves.

"Stop worrying," I order sternly.

"I can't help it, Marvin," Raymond replies. "It's Fats."

"Fats? What about Fats?"

"He's gone," says Raymond sadly.

"What do you mean?" I demand. Fats wouldn't go anywhere, not when our larder is full of cheese and hot pastrami-on-rye sandwiches and pickles and tortilla chips. Everything that he cares about in life is right here.

"Gone," repeats Raymond. "Disappeared. Vanished without a trace." I think I detect a tear or two in his eyes, fogging up his spectacles.

It's beginning to dawn on me that Raymond may be serious.

"Let me get this straight," I say, frowning. "Are you trying to tell me that Fats is not at this moment asleep in his bed upstairs?"

Raymond nods gravely.

"And you have no idea where he is?"

Raymond nods again.

"Why didn't you tell me this before?" I say. "This is serious. This is an emergency."

"I tried to tell you," Raymond answers. "But you wouldn't listen."

This is no time for bickering. We have to keep our heads. I take charge, as a true leader should.

"All right, Raymond," I tell him. "Pull yourself together and tell me exactly what happened."

Raymond sits up straight. He takes out his pocket handkerchief and wipes his eyes. "Well," he begins, "after you left, Fats said he was tired of playing games. He made himself a snack—I think it was a peanut butter and watermelon-pickle sandwich—and then he went to take his nap in the doll carriage. I challenged myself to a game of chess. It was a hard-fought game, and I guess I lost track of time. The next thing I knew, it was dinnertime and neither you nor Fats had come back. This seemed strange, especially for Fats. So I went to the window to check. And the doll carriage was gone."

"Hmmm," I say. "I see."

I think it over. There could be a simple explanation. "Maybe the carriage was moved," I suggest. "Maybe those salesladies got so bored that they re-arranged the doll furniture. Fats is such a sound sleeper, he'd never wake up."

Raymond shakes his head. "No, Marvin," he says. "I set up my binoculars and surveyed the entire floor. It is gone."

But I am on my feet.

"I'm going out to check," I announce. "Fats may not be lost after all. He may just be misplaced."

Out the door I go, pausing only to make sure the cop isn't lurking about. Then I'm off our shelf and swinging down to the floor below, hissing, "Psst, Fats!" into the darkness.

My inspection is fast and thorough. Within minutes I am back.

"Raymond," I report, "I'm afraid I have bad news. The folding doll stroller is there. The plaid doll buggy is there. But the Dolly-Deluxe doll carriage is missing."

"I knew it." Raymond has gone into his slump at the table again. "Marvin," he says, looking at me grimly. "We must face the truth, as painful as it is. Our friend Fats has been bought."

I nod. In my mind's eye I can see what happened. At the very moment I was performing on the high wire, Fats was being gift wrapped. And he probably slept right through it.

There is silence in our little house.

Then Raymond sniffs. "Poor Fats," he says softly. "Taken from his home, never to be seen again. A pathetic lost creature, so helpless, so small." His glasses are starting to fog up again.

"Small?" I put in. "I wouldn't exactly call him small."

But Raymond goes on. "He was always so kind, so

generous. He had a smile for everyone. And I don't believe I ever heard him utter an unkind word."

"That's because his mouth was too full," I mutter. But even I am beginning to feel a little downhearted. Without Fats our house seems too big. "Good old Fats," I say. "Just looking at him was always good for a laugh."

"Remember the time he was so busy looking at Santa Claus that he fell out the window?" Raymond asks.

"And the time he ate too many pickles and turned that funny shade of green?" I add.

"Good old Fats," sighs Raymond mournfully.

"Good old Fats," I echo. I am aware of a strange lump in my throat.

A lump in my throat? I, Merciless Marvin, tough guy?

This is ridiculous. This is unheard of. This has got to stop.

"Wait a minute," I say suddenly. "We're forgetting something."

"What are we forgetting?" asks Raymond.

I leap up on the table. I always think better when I am the center of attention. "We're forgetting who we are," I inform him. "Remember when Macy's Santa Claus was missing and the entire Police Department of the City of New York couldn't find him? Who was it who tracked Santa Claus down? Who was it who followed his trail through wind and cold and drifting snow all the way to Brooklyn? Who was it who figured out a way to outsmart his kidnaper and return Santa to the children of New York in time for Christmas?"

"We did," answers Raymond.

"Exactly," I say. "If we could do all that, finding Fats will be child's play. A snap. A pushover."

Raymond doesn't look so sure. He opens his mouth to say something, but I wave him quiet.

"Silence," I order. "A master detective is thinking."

Once again our house is still.

I pace the table, my nimble brain racing.

"I've got it!" I cry. "We'll use bloodhounds." This is the way it is always done in the movies. One whiff of the victim's clothing and the dogs are off, racing through the woods, the fields, the swamp, baying at the moon. In no time at all they've tracked him down.

28

Raymond is looking at me strangely.

"What's the matter?" I ask.

"I wonder," he says mildly, "if it is wise to send dogs after a mouse."

I consider. I think of baying at the moon. I think of long pink tongues dripping saliva. I think of teeth.

"I guess not," I decide.

I pace some more. My brain is in high gear now.

"I've got it!" I cry. "We'll advertise." This is also big in the movies. I can see it now. A poster with Fats's picture on it plastered on every street corner in the city. "Missing Person. Last seen in Macy's toy department. Height: 2 inches. Weight: 2 pounds. Answers to name Fats."

"Of course, we'll have to offer a reward," I add. "How much money have we got?"

Among all the other things he collects, Raymond saves the coins that roll under the counter beyond the reach of the salesclerks.

"A dollar and eighty-seven cents," says Raymond.

"Is that all?" I was thinking of $500. But for Fats, maybe $1.87 is enough.

Raymond is frowning again.

"Marvin," he says, "I think you are forgetting one thing. Fats is not a missing person but a misssing mouse. It is a sad-but-true fact of life that when you are a mouse, you can't afford to advertise. Who knows who might answer the ad? It could be an exterminator."

I shudder at the thought. And go back to my pacing.

I notice that Raymond has stopped moping and is sitting up straight, twirling his whiskers. This is a sure sign that he is thinking.

"Yes," he mumbles to himself. "It just might work."

"What might work?" I demand.

"The cash register slip," he replies.

I don't know what he is talking about. I think he has slipped *his* register.

"The cash register slip is the store's record of a sale," Raymond explains. "When a customer buys something, the salesclerk makes out a slip, gives the customer a copy, and keeps the other copy in the register."

I know all of this. I haven't been watching salesclerks all these months for nothing. But I still don't know what it has to do with Fats.

"My idea is this," Raymond goes on patiently. "I happen to know that today's sales slips are still in the register. They will be picked up in the morning. If we could look at them, we might be able to find out if someone bought a doll carriage today. Better yet, if it was a charge account customer, we could find out the buyer's name and address."

Now I get it. And I have to admit it's not a bad idea. In fact, it could be the clue we need to crack this case.

"Raymond, old boy," I say, "you just may have something."

I jump off the table. But in midair a thought hits me. "Hold everything. How do we get into this register?"

"Don't worry about that," Raymond says. He has taken out his notebook and is busily scribbling notes. "Just leave everything to me."

I had almost forgotten. When we lived in the movie theater, Raymond used to spend hours reading old magazines people left under the seats. His favorite was *Popular Mechanics*. He is a mechanical marvel.

Leaping into the air, I click my heels together. I've always wanted to crack a safe. A cash register will be almost as good.

"What are we waiting for?" I cry. "Let's go crack the cash register!"

3

I Crack a Cash Register

"What are we waiting for?" I call impatiently.

"Just a minute, Marvin." Raymond's voice is muffled, as if it were coming from inside a bureau drawer. Which is probably where he is. He's been upstairs gathering together his cash-register-cracking equipment, while I keep watch at the front door for the cop. The cop has come and made his rounds and gone, and still I wait. One thing you have to say about Raymond: He may be thorough, but he's slow.

"Raymond," I call again.

There is a thump and a small crash. "Coming, Marvin."

A moment later Raymond appears. He looks like an undernourished miniature Santa Claus. Over his shoulder is slung a bulging sack—really a red mitten from Raymond's collection of lost mittens— and from it protrudes the weirdest assortment of wires and springs and rubber bands and paper clips and odd objects that I've ever seen.

"Are you sure you have everything?" I ask. The mitten is so full, it looks like it might explode.

"Well . . ." Raymond looks a little doubtful. "I couldn't find my long-nosed pliers. But I think I can do the job without them."

"Then let's get cracking," I order.

I take a quick peek out the door. Nothing seems to be stirring. The dim light from the one bulb that burns in the toy department at night shines on the cash register that is our goal.

"The coast is clear," I hiss over my shoulder.

I leap expertly to the shelf below. Raymond lowers his sack, clinking and clanking in the still- ness, into my arms. "Sssh," I tell it. Then Raymond climbs down, and I hand the sack to him. A few more of these maneuvers and we've done it. We're standing on the counter next to the cash register.

I look it over. I have to admit that it looks tough to crack. It is one of these new machines, sleek and smooth and smart-looking. And it seems to have a mind of its own. When Mrs. O'Grady operates it, lights flash and the machinery inside grumbles and growls. After a lot of complaining from both of them, it finally spits out a piece of paper. But sometimes, if it's not in the mood, it refuses to do anything at all. Then we can hear Mrs. O'Grady running to find the manager of the toy department. "Oh, Mr. Peterson," she calls. "It's that Machine again." I know that even I, Merciless Marvin the Magnificent, wouldn't want to tangle with this cash register. I hope Raymond knows what he is doing.

Raymond looks calm and confident. He is busily unpacking his sack, laying out his equipment on the counter beside him. There are all kinds of wires— fat and thin, long and short, twisted and straight. There's even a fat, curled-up copper one that is Raymond's special favorite: He removed it from a mousetrap in the days when we lived in the movie theater, and has been saving it ever since. Then there are springs and screws and safety pins and bits of metal salvaged from broken toys, several flashlight batteries, a can opener, a pocket comb, a couple of magnets, a set of miniature tools from a Junior Handyman set, and a bag of salted peanuts.

"What are those for?" I ask, pointing to the peanuts.

"This may take a little while," Raymond answers. "You know what Fats would say—we have to keep our strength up."

At the mention of Fats's name a cloud seems to descend over him. "Poor Fats," he sighs. "He may have eaten his last salted peanut. He may be lying dead in an alley somewhere."

I shiver. But I know we can't afford to think gloomy thoughts. Not if we are going to succeed in this rescue operation. We have to think positive. "Nonsense!" I reply. "Probably he's only unconscious. And if that's the case, we've got to move fast."

"You're right, Marvin," says Raymond. And shaking his head, he snaps out of it.

He selects a screwdriver from his array of tools. Then he walks all the way around the cash register, poking here, pressing there. He reminds me of a doctor looking over a patient. I wouldn't be surprised if he took its temperature.

After a few minutes of this, Raymond steps back, rubbing his paws together. "Very interesting," he says.

"Can you do it?" I ask eagerly.

"I'm not sure yet," replies Raymond.

Now he goes into action with his wires and magnets and batteries. The cash register begins to resemble something from outer space, with wires draped all over it and springs sticking up in odd places. Raymond, wearing wires around his neck and his screwdriver behind one ear, looks like a mad scientist. It's hard to tell if he's going to crack open this register or send it off to another planet.

Whatever he does, it looks like it will take a little while. So I pull up a stuffed cat to use as a pillow and relax. I reach for the salted peanuts, toss a couple in the air, and catch them in my mouth. Just keeping my strength up.

My strength is way up, and I'm feeling so comfortable that I'm about to doze off, when suddenly I hear a low humming noise. My eyes pop open.

There is Raymond on top of the register, a magnet in one paw, wires wrapped around his entire body, doing a strange little dance. "I think I've got it, Marvin!" he cries excitedly. The humming noise grows louder. And louder. Either he's got it, or the register is about to explode. Now there is a series of loud clanking sounds, a kind of groan, and lights begin to flash. The whole machine is vibrating. It's going to go up in smoke.

"Run for your life, Raymond!" I shout.

And then, just as I'm certain the end has come, the cash register drawer pops open.

Raymond moves his magnet aside. The lights stop flashing. The clanking sounds grow softer, then stop. The machine subsides.

"We did it!" I exclaim. I have to admit I'm a little surprised.

Raymond coils up his wires, unhooks his batteries, and hands everything down to me. Then he jumps down, giving the register an affectionate pat in passing. "Nothing to it," he says with a touch of pride. "You just have to have the right equipment."

I'm already peering into the open drawer. "There

are sales slips," I report. "A whole pile of them. I didn't think they made that many sales."

I jump into the drawer and start looking through them. Only I can't see a thing. "Help! It's dark in here."

"Just a minute, Marvin." Raymond reaches into his sack and brings out a pocket flashlight. He hands it to me. Then, notebook and pencil in hand, he climbs into the drawer.

I shine the light on the top slip. " 'Gx123tr-xyz-gltz-zork,' " I read out loud. What is this? Doesn't this machine speak English?

Raymond is the big reader. I pass the slip to him.

He reads the second line. " 'A246-trnx 98765-bpfff.' Hmm, sounds like computer language. These new registers are pretty complicated." He examines the rest of the slip. "It's all printed in some kind of code that only a computer can understand."

Raymond sounds dejected. Can it be that only the computer knows who bought Fats?

Now he is shining his light on the bottom right-hand corner. "Wait a minute!" he says excitedly. "Yes, here it is. We've been saved by Mrs. O'Grady. She doesn't believe in this new register and all its codes and numbers. She still uses good old-fashioned handwriting."

Raymond squints through his spectacles. "Her writing is kind of hard to make out. I think it says 'Raggedy Ann doll.' "

" 'Raggedy Ann doll,' " I repeat. "That's not it. Look at the next slip."

The next slip says "Doll clothes."

"That doesn't sound like Fats," I decide.

And then: "Doll high chair." And: "Baby Bubbles and Cuddles." And: "Raggedy Andy."

"Keep going," I tell Raymond. There are only two slips left.

Raymond frowns. "This one is really hard to make out," he says. " 'Doll carpet.' No. 'Doll cabbage.' No. Marvin, this is it! It says 'Doll carriage.' "

"Let me see that." I look over Raymond's shoulder. Mrs. O'Grady's writing is terrible, all right. It looks like she was bitten by a bee while writing up the sale. Or maybe she saw a mouse. But there's no doubt that it says "Doll carriage."

"We've found Fats!" I cheer. "Didn't I tell you it would be a pushover? It's all in a day's work for a master detective."

"We haven't quite found him yet," Raymond reminds me. "But I think we may have found out who has him."

"Who does?"

Raymond is carefully copying something in his little notebook. He finishes writing, double-checks it, then looks up at me.

"The customer who bought the doll carriage," he says, "is Dr. Henry Simpson, Apartment Nine F, Nine Ninety-nine Fifth Avenue, New York City."

4
I Travel Uptown

"We can't do it, Marvin. I tell you, it's too dangerous. We'll be squashed flat. Or thrown out on our ear. Or arrested."

"Nonsense," I reply. "I do it all the time."

It's the next afternoon. We are standing at the bus stop, waiting for the bus, when Raymond has this attack of cold feet. I'd forgotten that he is not used to lurking and slinking and darting around town like me. He spends his time sitting around thinking. I can see I'm going to have to give him a pep talk.

"Look, Raymond," I begin. "Buses are easy. Not quite as easy as the subway, maybe, because of that big step up. But there's nothing to it, really. All we have to do is hitch a ride. I've traveled by handbag, briefcase, and umbrella. Once I even rode in a man's pant cuff." I have to admit that was a little nerve-racking, even for me. "But shopping bags are easier. For a beginner, I suggest a shopping bag."

Raymond still looks doubtful. Terrified is more like it.

I cheer him on. "Raymond, old boy, you've got to have courage! Fortitude! Muscles of iron and nerves of steel! Like me. Remember your name."

"Raymond the Rat?"

"Exactly." I gave Raymond his name back in the old days in the Bijou Theater, when I was training him to be part of my gang. It was supposed to make him think tough. It worked then. I molded Raymond, a dreamy bookworm of a mouse, into a crafty, conniving criminal, my right-hand man. With his help, and the inspiration of the hundreds of gangster movies we'd watched, I was able to pull off my first big job—robbing a cheese store. But

44

Raymond tends to forget. He was not born tough, like me.

Raymond tries a tough expression. He looks like he has a touch of indigestion.

But I don't have time now to worry about Raymond. An old lady, kind of bent over and slow moving, has just appeared on the scene. And she is carrying two shopping bags. The perfect target. At the same time I see a bus approaching.

Digging Raymond in the ribs, I hiss in his ear, "Do what I do. Move fast and don't ask questions."

I choose the paper shopping bag rather than the plastic one. In case of emergency, you can always chew your way out. Up and over, and I drop lightly into the bag. I wait for Raymond. Seconds later he comes crashing down on top of me.

"Look before you jump," I growl at him.

"Sorry, Marvin," he whispers.

But we're in the bag, and it's moving. Up the steps, very slowly, and we hear change clinking. More movement, and then suddenly—*plunk*—the bag is set down hard. Raymond lands on top of me again.

I glare at him.

"Sorry, Marvin," he whispers again. At least it's not Fats sitting on my stomach.

He gets off. I can hear the old lady settling creakily into a seat.

"What do we do now?" asks Raymond.

"Now we relax," I say, "and enjoy the ride."

I look around me, checking out this bag. I've ridden in a lot of shopping bags in my time, and I know there are good ones and bad ones. Bags from the hardware store are usually bad. They're full of sharp edges—coat hangers, screwdrivers, and tacks. Bags from dress shops are good, a little boring but a nice soft ride. Bags from bakeries and delicatessens are always delicious. You get a free meal along with a free ride. Bags from department stores can be bad —lampshades and egg beaters—or good—goose-down pillows and cashmere sweaters. Probably the worst bag I ever rode in was a knitting bag. Being wrapped up in wool and bounced on knitting needles is not a restful experience. The best bag I ever rode in was a bag of Boston cream pies.

This one is a mixed bag, I decide. It's got soap

and toothpaste, hand lotion, tissues, a couple of jars of vitamins, a hair net ("Stay away from the hair net," I warn Raymond. "It's like a sneaky mouse-trap."), some sewing things, an old sweater, two library books, and a little bag of peppermints.

I help myself to a mint. It's so minty, it takes my breath away. While I frantically fan my mouth, Raymond is checking the titles of the library books. *"The Case of the Cranky Cat,"* he reads. "Hmm, I've never read that one."

Raymond loves mysteries. If he starts reading, we'll be on this bus till the end of the line.

"We've got no time for reading," I tell him quickly. "We may be getting off soon. I'm going to check."

This is the risky part about traveling by shopping bag. The bag you're in may not be going where you want to go. Usually I'm not too fussy. But this time we have a destination. Raymond has figured out that 999 Fifth Avenue is right across the street from the Metropolitan Museum of Art. So we want to get off the bus at 81st Street.

I make my way to the top of the bag. Concealing

myself in the folds of the old lady's sweater, I peer out. I'm looking for a street sign. But though I crane my neck, I can't even see a window. All I can see is legs. Trouser legs, knee-sock legs, blue-jean legs. This bus is crowded.

I don't panic. I've traveled during rush hour before. I keep cool and listen. Sure enough, after a minute I hear someone ask, "What street is this, anyway?" And someone else replies, "Seventy-second, I think."

We're fast approaching our stop. And so far the old lady shows no signs of getting off. I can see that we may have to pull one of my trickier maneuvers. We may have to switch bags.

I alert Raymond. He comes struggling up over the lotion bottle and joins me in the sweater.

"Are we there?" he asks.

"Almost," I say.

But when I tell him my plan for getting off the bus, his nerves of steel have a complete collapse.

"Did you see how many legs are out there?" he asks, his voice quavering. "Those legs have feet on the ends of them. We'll be crushed into crumbs like a couple of animal crackers. It's too dangerous."

"Courage, Raymond the Rat," I remind him.

But he's shaking like a leaf. In fact, he's shaking so hard, I can feel the whole bag moving. "Stop that," I order.

And then I realize it isn't Raymond who is making the bag move. It's the old lady. We're in luck. She's getting off the bus after all.

"Hang on to your hat!" I tell Raymond happily.

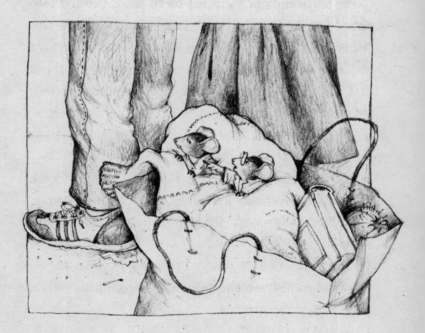

Bounce, bounce, bounce. I'm wrapped snugly in the sweater. *Jounce, jounce.* I slip out and hit the hard corner of a library book. And then, *bump.* I land bottom first on something sharp. "Ouch!" I yelp. I'm being stuck with tacks, poked with pins, pierced with a hundred needles.

"Help!" I call. Where is Raymond? I've got to get off this bed of nails.

"Courage, Marvin." Raymond appears, calmly munching on a mint. "It's only a pincushion."

He helps me up. I grit my teeth as he extracts two pins from my left hind leg and three from my tail. When he's finished, I feel as full of holes as a piece of Swiss cheese. But there is no time to worry about that. I can tell by the sounds and the cold air that we're off the bus. It's time to get out of this bag.

"Follow me," I hiss at Raymond. "When I say jump, jump."

Up to the top of the bag I climb. I take a quick look around for ferocious dogs, cops, and other dangers. The coast seems clear. And the bag is traveling slowly.

"Jump!"

I land nimbly on the sidewalk. Seconds later Raymond comes crashing down on top of me.

"Sorry, Marvin," he says for the third time that day.

"Raymond, old boy," I mutter under my breath, "Next time remind me to let you jump first."

I struggle to my feet and look around. We're on a corner under a streetlight. Next to it is a sign. "Madison Av" it says on one side. And "E 79 St" on the other.

We've done it. Well, almost. We still have two or three blocks to walk.

"This way to Fifth Avenue," I tell Raymond. And I proceed to show him how a mouse of the streets lurks and slinks and darts around town.

Raymond follows me, breathing hard. Every once in a while I hear him call weakly, "Marvin, wait for me."

At last I take pity on him and slow down.

"Here we are," I announce. "Fifth Avenue."

Across the street I can make out a huge building with fancy columns and millions of steps, and behind it a lot of trees. This, I know, is Central Park. Raymond stops panting. He is gazing at the building with a look of wonder. "The Metropolitan Museum of Art," he sighs. He says it the way Fats speaks of cheese. "If only . . ."

"If only what?" I ask.

"If only we could peek inside," he says dreamily.

"We can't," I snap. "Have you forgotten our mission?"

"Our mission. Of course, our mission." Raymond snaps out of his trance. Taking out his notebook, he is all business. "We are looking for 999 Fifth Avenue." He looks up at the nearest building. "This is 973. It must be about two more blocks."

So we proceed up Fifth Avenue. 977, 985, 991. I notice that this is a fancy neighborhood in which Dr. Henry Simpson lives. The buildings are big and old and have canopies over the front doors, and little trees in pots, and doormen. We stay close to the curb so we won't be seen.

We are crossing 81st Street when I spot it. It's in the middle of the next block, a tall gray building with a tower on top like a castle. A blue canopy stretches from the building to the curb. And on the side of the canopy, in swirling gold letters, it says: "Nine Ninety Nine."

I pinch Raymond. He nods. He has seen it too.

It's time to go undercover. We dart from curb to trash can to mailbox and finally into a long low hedge that lines the front of the building. This provides perfect camouflage. We make our way inside the hedge until it ends, right next to the front door.

Pushing aside some leaves, I peer out. Again we're in luck. Not only does the hedge provide camouflage, but an observation post as well. Raymond joins me, notebook in hand.

So this is it. The place where our friend Fats may well be being held captive. If he is still alive.

I can tell Raymond has the same thought. "Are you up there, Fats?" he whispers softly, his whiskers trembling.

I have to admit it is a formidable-looking building. Up close it looks like a fortress, with all that gray stone and the iron bars on the front doors and a doorman in a blue uniform that matches the canopy, standing guard at the door like a soldier. Getting inside is not going to be easy.

However, it can be done. Didn't I single-handedly engineer the greatest cheese robbery of our time? Didn't I travel all the way to the wilds of Brooklyn to save a snatched Santa Claus? I am equal to this challenge.

We remain at our observation post a long time. Not surprisingly, since we are next to a door, we observe a lot of coming and going. Taxis coming and limousines going and people with briefcases coming and people in evening clothes going and shopping bags from Saks Fifth Avenue coming and poodles wearing diamond collars going. We learn that the doorman's name is George ("Good evening, sir." "Good evening, George.") and that he is very large. Raymond duly takes note of all of this in his notebook. We do not see either a Dolly-Deluxe doll carriage or a stout mouse answering to the name Fats.

At last I have seen enough.

Poking Raymond, I say, "Let's go home."

He nods, closing his notebook.

"Marvin," he says hesitantly, "traveling by shopping bag was—uh—interesting, but all in all I think I prefer the subway. Can we take the IRT?"

"Why not?" I reply.

5

I Come Up with a Plan

"Here is the plan," I tell Raymond.

It is later that night, and we are sitting around the kitchen table having a midnight snack of Corn Doodles and discussing our next move. One thing about Fats being missing, the Corn Doodles last a lot longer.

"We disguise ourselves as delivery men and toss a smoke bomb into the lobby," I say. "Then, while everybody is coughing and choking, we slip inside." Fats would love this. His favorite part in the movies was always when something blew up. That's how I happened to give him his name, Fats the Fuse.

Raymond frowns thoughtfully. "If everyone is coughing and choking," he observes, "we'll be coughing and choking too."

"Gas masks," I say, thinking fast. "We wear gas masks."

"Where do we get them?" Raymond asks. "They don't sell gas masks at Macy's. Not to mention the difficulty of finding our size."

"Okay, okay," I mutter. "You don't like that idea, here's another one. We don't bother with the front door at all. Instead we attack from the air. We hire a plane and parachute down to the roof of the building. In the dark of night when there is no moon, of course." I think I like this idea even better. I saw it done in a war movie once. The soldiers parachuted behind enemy lines and stormed the castle where the enemy general had his headquarters. It was terrific.

"That sounds—uh—exciting," says Raymond. "But I wonder if we need to go to so much trouble."

"Trouble? It's no trouble," I answer. My imagination is shifting into high gear. I can see it all now. I check with my pilot, he circles low over the build-

ing, and at the signal I jump. Down, down, down I
tumble, head over heels through space, traveling
faster than any mouse has ever traveled. And then
—at the last possible second—I pull the cord to
open my parachute. Silently, invisibly, I float down
to the rooftop. It will be terrific. I've done a lot of
daring things in my career, but I've never jumped
out of a plane. I can't wait to try it.

Raymond's voice pierces my daydream. "Marvin,"
he is saying. "Be sensible."

Sensible. That's the trouble with Raymond. He is
always sensible. If I listen to him, I'll never fly.

I won't listen.

"It's a brilliant idea," I tell him.

"Pardon me for saying so," says Raymond, "but it's crazy."

"It's daring," I say.

"It's foolhardy," says Raymond.

"It's clever," I say.

"It's—uh—dumb," says Raymond.

"It can't fail," I say.

"It'll never fly," says Raymond.

He has an answer for everything.

"Where do we get this plane?" he goes on. "And the parachutes? How do we spot the building from above? How do we manage to land on the roof instead of on some sharp church steeple or tangled in the treetops in Central Park?"

"Details, details," I mumble. But Raymond has done it again. He has brought me down to earth.

"I'm sorry, Marvin," he says, offering the bag of Corn Doodles as a consolation prize. "It's just that often the strategies that work in the movies don't work in real life. Especially when you're a mouse. I have found that for a mouse it is best to think small."

I take a pawful of Corn Doodles and try to think

small. For a mouse of my vision and imagination, it's not easy. Maybe if I had a bit of caviar to spread on my Corn Doodles, it might help. Besides being my favorite taste treat, it's good for the brain. But the last time we raided the delicatessen, the caviar was all sold out.

Crunch, crunch, crunch. I munch and rack my brain. *Crunch, crunch, crunch.* Raymond munches and reviews his notes.

A few minutes later I notice that only one of us is munching. Raymond is writing furiously in his notebook.

I wait. At last he stops writing and looks up. "Marvin," he says quietly, "I think I may have a plan."

"Yes?" I am willing to listen.

"As you know," Raymond begins, "I made a detailed study of Nine Ninety-nine Fifth Avenue today. The type of construction, the size and structural soundness of the door, that kind of thing. After careful consideration I have reached the conclusion that the major obstacle to getting inside is the doorman."

"George," I say.

"George," says Raymond.

I nod. I came to this conclusion myself, without taking notes.

"He is big," Raymond continues. "He is strong. And he takes his job seriously. It is my opinion that anyone attempting to enter the building who does not belong would be bounced out on his ear."

I nod again. A tough customer, this George. A major obstacle.

"Nevertheless"—Raymond pauses dramatically —"I think he has a weakness."

I'm all ears. I can't imagine what it is. A glass jaw maybe? I'm pretty sure it's not that he is an animal lover.

"He is neat," says Raymond.

"Neat?" I repeat. I don't get it.

Raymond nods. "While we were watching him, I observed that he likes everything just so. His shoes are shined, the buttons on his uniform are shined, the knobs on the front door are shined. And if anything is dropped on the sidewalk, he picks it up and puts it in the trash basket."

This is true. But I still don't understand Raymond's point.

Raymond opens his notebook to a page on which he has drawn a complicated diagram, full of *x*'s and *o*'s and little arrows pointing here and there. "This is us," he informs me, pointing to two *x*'s near the bottom of the page. "And this is him." He points to a big *O*. "Now. We station ourselves exactly where we were tonight. We have with us some bits of paper, maybe an old Corn Doodles bag or a candy wrapper. This is the bait." He points to another *x*. "We drop the bait on the sidewalk, right about here. George the doorman leaves his position at the door to pick it up. As he does we leave our hiding place." Raymond points to two arrows. "He goes this way, to the trash basket. We go that way, to the door. And that's it. We're inside."

Now I understand. My first reaction is that Raymond sure knows how to think small. His plan has no disguises, no fancy equipment, no explosions, no jumping out of planes—none of the dashing, daring, dangerous deeds I love. It is like Raymond: sensible. One might even say boring.

On the other hand the plan has a certain simplicity that I like. There are no disguises to assemble, no fancy equipment to go wrong, no explosives to blow up in our faces. All we need is ourselves—and a little garbage. And it is a plan that can be put into effect immediately. That is important, when Fats's life may be at stake.

"Okay, Raymond," I say, coming to a swift decision like a good leader should. "We'll try it."

6

I Encounter an Unexpected Development

"Taxi!" I call, waving my paw at a bright yellow cab.

But it turns the corner without seeing me.

"Taxi?" Raymond drags me out of the street. "Marvin, what are you thinking of?"

I'm thinking of traveling in style, that's what I'm thinking of. If these people on Fifth Avenue can do it, so can I.

"It's the only way to travel," I inform Raymond. "Buses, the subway—that's dull, ordinary stuff. We're moving up."

Raymond shakes his head slowly. "Marvin," he says, "I don't think my nerves will take it."

I look him over. I note a tremble in his whiskers, a twitch in his tail. I'm afraid it's true. He can't take another adventure like our bus trip. He'll fall apart before we even get to 999 Fifth Avenue.

"Okay, okay," I grumble. "We'll take the subway."

But as we duck down the stairs to the BMT, I promise myself that someday I, Merciless Marvin the Magnificent, will travel only by taxi.

We manage the subway with the ease of experience. First we station ourselves inconspicuously behind a pillar near the end of the platform. When the train pulls in, we wait until the doors are about to close. Then we hop on board the last car. Usually it's empty. But even when it's not, during rush hour, people are too busy trying to get a seat or a strap to hang on to to look down. It's easy. Boringly easy.

The only trouble with going by subway is that we have to change trains and then walk about seven blocks to get to our destination. "A taxi takes you door to door," I remind Raymond as we trudge across Park Avenue. Raymond does not reply.

Finally that awning with the number "Nine Ninety Nine" comes into view. Again we duck into the hedge and make our way through its dark leafy tunnel until we reach our observation post. Immediately I peek out to survey the scene.

The scene is the same as yesterday. The same plush blue and gold, the same iron-barred doors. And the same immense doorman, standing at attention at the door. I notice that Raymond was right. Everything about George the doorman, from the gold braid of his hat to the gleaming black of his shoes, shines. All he needs is a few medals on his chest and he'd look like the enemy general in my favorite war movie.

While I am looking things over, Raymond is unpacking his knapsack, borrowed from a doll called Sporty Sam, Ace Adventurer. Raymond has come prepared, as usual. In the knapsack he has all the equipment we could need. There is his notebook, of course. And a couple of empty candy bar wrappers. We chose Snickers, Fats's all-time favorite. Then, for the rescue operation, Raymond has brought along his standard rescue-operation equipment: a key ring containing about sixteen keys (Raymond's lifetime collection), a coil of string from a yo-yo (for scaling walls and lassoing things), a Boy Scout pocket knife (three blades, a can opener, and a nail file, useful in case we have to saw through steel bars to reach Fats), a pocket flashlight (for signaling and sneaking around in the dark of night), and a Sporty Sam plastic machete. Raymond is also ready for any emergency. There is our emergency disguise —a tattered man's handkerchief with the initial *G* in the corner, perfect for throwing over ourselves in case we are spotted. There is our emergency escape kit—a little bag of marbles that we can toss at an enemy's feet, tripping him while we make our escape. And finally there is our emergency weapon—a little envelope containing Raymond's special blend of pepper, hot spices, dust, and imported hayseeds, that is guaranteed to make an enemy sneeze when thrown in his face. We are ready for anything.

Raymond checks over all of this to make sure it is in working order, then repacks the knapsack.

"Ready?" I ask impatiently. Now that the rescue operation is finally underway, I can't wait for a little action.

"Almost," says Raymond. "I'm just making sure

our emergency equipment is where we can reach it in an emergency."

A moment later he announces, "Ready, Marvin."

He hands me a Snickers wrapper.

I inspect it. I crumple it up a little more around the edges. It looks like garbage, all right.

Now Raymond extends his paw outside the hedge.

"What are you doing?" I ask.

"Checking the wind," Raymond answers. "We can't have the bait blow away before the doorman has time to pick it up."

He brings his paw inside. "Just as I thought. There is a slight breeze. It's best not to take any chances." He fishes around in the bottom of the knapsack until he comes up with a blue marble. He wraps the Snickers wrapper around it. "There," he says. "That should add just enough weight to do the trick."

We move to the edge of the hedge closest to the sidewalk. "Placement of the bait is very important," Raymond goes on. "It must be far enough away to give us time to reach the door, yet not so far that the doorman won't notice it. I think right about there."

Raymond points to a crack in the middle of the sidewalk, directly in front of the building.

I nod. "Nothing to it," I say.

"Are you sure you can do it?" Raymond asks, looking worried.

"Is Fats fat? Of course, I can do it." I am the speediest sprinter around. I've outrun cats, rats, movie ushers, Macy's salesclerks, cops, even an irate French chef with a meat cleaver in his hand. This is going to be child's play.

Raymond hands me the Snickers wrapper. He checks the sidewalk, to the left and to the right. "All clear," he reports. "All right, Marvin. On your mark. Get set. Go!"

Zip. I dart to the crack in the middle of the sidewalk. I drop the Snickers wrapper. *Zip.* I dart back inside the hedge. It's over in five seconds, and I'm not even winded.

Now we turn to watch George the doorman. He is holding his hat in his hand, fingering the gold braid. He appears to be trying to polish its threads.

"Come on," I mutter. "Look up."

Almost as if he has heard me, he glances toward the sidewalk. A frown suddenly creases his forehead. He puts his hat back on his head. Then he takes a step toward the bait.

"Now!"

We're off and running for the door. Our timing is perfect. It's just like the little arrows in Raymond's diagram. As the doorman goes one way, we go the other. In about five seconds more it's all over. We're inside.

But before I have time to congratulate myself on the smooth execution of my plan, there is an unexpected development. In fact, there are three unexpected developments, one right after another.

The first is the darkness. After the bright sunshine outside, the lobby is dim. We can't see a thing. We stop and blink, trying to get our bearings, trying to locate the elevators.

Finally I spot them, behind some potted palms along the back wall. But then comes the second unexpected development: the carpet. Like everything else, it is blue and gold, and the pile is so deep that we sink right into it. It's like quicksand. Each time we take a step, we sink in up to our noses. I can't believe it. Here we are, in the lobby of 999 Fifth Avenue at last, and we're caught in the carpet.

"Help!" calls Raymond, disappearing completely from sight.

"Quiet," I command.

This is a tight spot. We are still in the doorway, in position to be trampled to death by anyone going in or out. We have to act fast.

I get down on all fours and try slithering between the strands of the rug, like an African hunter moving through tall grass in the movies. It works. "Follow me," I hiss at Raymond. We both slither. Moments later we bump our noses on cold marble floor.

"Whew!" I stand up, mopping my brow. I feel like I've slithered across an entire African plain.

And that's when I confront the third development. This one is truly revolting. It is standing next to the elevator and is wearing the same kind of blue uniform as the doorman. It can only be the elevator man.

Not only that, but he is looking right at us.

"Raymond," I say in a low voice, "don't look now, but it's an emergency."

I have to say this much for Raymond—he doesn't panic. He reaches right into his Sporty Sam knapsack and comes out with our emergency disguise.

"Stand still," he whispers as he throws the handkerchief over us. I stand so still, I don't even breathe. Out of the corner of my eye I see that Raymond is holding our emergency weapon in his other paw, just in case.

For several seconds nothing happens. I dare to take a breath. And then I hear footsteps coming toward us across the marble floor.

"Get ready to fire," I warn Raymond. He opens the top of the envelope.

The footsteps come closer. And closer.

"This is it," I tell myself. Any second now the elevator man will lean over and snatch off our disguise.

And then there is one more unexpected development. I feel something push me from behind— something rough and scratchy, something that nearly knocks me off my feet.

"What is it?" cries Raymond.

I don't know. My brain struggles to figure out what is happening while my legs struggle to stay upright.

And then everything collapses. I land on my tail and Raymond lands on top of me and the envelope

goes flying and we're all wrapped up in the hand-kerchief, sliding across the floor. And the air is full of pepper and hot spices and dust and hayseeds.

"Ah-ah-ah-*choo!*" sneezes Raymond.

"Ah-ah-ah-ah-*choo!*" I sneeze. "Hang on!"

For now I realize what is happening. That prickly pushing thing is a broom, and we're being swept out of the building like a piece of garbage.

We hang on, bumping and sliding and sneezing and wheezing. And then, at last, it is over. I am dimly aware of cool air and a sudden stillness. I struggle to sit up, but I cannot. I just lie there, a bruised and battered pile of shivering, shaking, sniffling misery.

7

I Learn
Some Shocking News

"Imagine that," says Raymond, shaking his head. "A neat doorman *and* a neat elevator man. I can't get over it."

"Mmmmft," I mutter. What I can't get over is where we ended up yesterday. Not back on Fifth Avenue, but in an alley behind the building, with all the garbage. It wasn't dignified. It wasn't tough. It was downright humiliating.

I'm also having trouble getting over my bruises. I'm lying in bed with an ice pack on my nose (too much sneezing) and one on my tail (too much bouncing). I feel like my whole body should be on ice. This is worse than falling off the high wire.

"Oh, my aching nose," I moan softly.

"Can I get you anything, Marvin?" asks Raymond from my rocking chair. He has a Band-Aid on his left ear but is otherwise intact, probably because he had me as a cushion.

I shake my head, which causes all my bruises to ache and the ice pack to fall off my nose. I grit my teeth. Tough guys don't cry.

Raymond replaces the ice pack on my nose. "Lie still," he advises. "I'll read to you."

He picks up the *New York Globe,* which one of the salesclerks discards each morning in a certain trash can, and starts reading the headlines. " 'Man Bites Dog at Madison Square Garden.' 'Runaway Garbage Truck Lands in East River.' 'Million-Dollar Jewel Theft at World Trade Center. Thieves Escape by Parachute.' "

My ears prick up at that. As a former criminal, I like to keep up with what's happening in crime. "Read that one," I direct Raymond.

But Raymond doesn't seem to be listening. He's got his head buried in a story on page two.

"Read about the jewel theft," I tell him again, more sharply.

Raymond still doesn't look up. "Tsk, tsk," he mutters to himself. "Who would have believed it?" And a moment later, "Oh, my! Simply shocking."

"What is simply shocking?" I demand.

Raymond looks up at last. "Man's inhumanity to mouse," he says gravely. "Just look at this, Marvin."

He holds up a photograph. I can't quite make it out. I lean closer—and flinch. I've disturbed a delicate portion of my tail.

"Oh, my aching tail," I groan softly.

"Sorry, Marvin." Raymond brings the newspaper closer. I can make out rows of cages, and inside them some small creatures. It looks suspiciously like mice behind bars.

"Tsk, tsk." I shake my head.

"That's not all," says Raymond indignantly. "Wait till you hear the story." He moves the newspaper back under his nose and reads: " 'Doctors Accused of Cruelty in Laboratory Tests. Experiments on Mice Stir Up Controversy at Local Hospital.' That's the headline."

"Tests? What kind of tests?" I interrupt him to ask.

"Medical tests," replies Raymond. "It says here that these doctors try out new medicines on mice before giving them to people. First they make the mice sick. Then they give them the medicine and watch to see if they get better or worse." Raymond takes off his spectacles and wipes away a tear. "Oh, it's terrible. Just terrible."

"Cruel," I agree. I myself wouldn't stand for it. I'd spit the medicine out.

"But the really cruel part," Raymond goes on, "is the way they treat these mice, who never did anything to anybody, who are serving mankind so nobly. There are five hundred of them, crowded into small cages without light or air, the article says. And sometimes they don't feed them for several days."

"You're right," I say. "It is shocking."

I try to imagine what it would be like to be locked up in a cage, without light or air or food. I couldn't take it. I would stage a jailbreak.

Raymond puts his spectacles back on his nose and reads on. "It says: 'The American Society for the Prevention of Cruelty to Animals and other groups are planning protest demonstrations at the offices of the two doctors involved, Dr. William Frost and Dr.—' Good grief!" Raymond clutches his throat, as if he's just swallowed some bad medicine, and drops the newspaper.

"Dr. Goodgrief?" I repeat. "That's a strange name."

Raymond is struggling to get ahold of himself.

"The name of the second doctor," he says in a low choked voice, "is Dr. Henry Simpson."

Dr. Henry Simpson. That name sounds familiar. Where have I heard it before? "You don't mean—" I sit up. "You can't mean—"

Raymond nods grimly. "Yes, Marvin. It appears as if our friend Fats has fallen into the hands of a doctor who tortures mice."

I slump back on my pillow. I can't believe it. This is too revolting a development. And yet in my mind's eye I can see it all clearly. Fats behind bars. Fats being fed medicine. Fats not being fed food. Fats getting thinner and thinner. Fats fading away. Fats not being Fats anymore.

"No!" I shout suddenly. "I won't stand for it!" I leap out of bed, scattering ice in all directions.

Raymond looks at me in amazement. "But, Marvin," he says. "Your aching nose. Your aching tail."

"Never mind my nose and tail," I snap. "I've never felt better in my life." And to prove it I jump in the air, click my heels together, and do a double somersault to the floor. "Now, then," I say. "This Dr. Henry Simpson can have those other mice. They don't know what it's like to live free and see the world and taste Wisconsin cheddar cheese and watermelon pickles and caviar. They probably like the flavor of that medicine he feeds them. But he can't have Fats. No!"

"No!" echoes Raymond.

"We are going to rescue Fats from the clutches of this deadly doctor!" I shout.

"Right!" cries Raymond. He is beginning to catch my spirit. He puts down his newspaper and waves his fist in the air.

"And," I proclaim quietly, "we are going to do it today."

8

I Take Part in a Demonstration

So once again we've taken up our position inside the hedge at 999 Fifth Avenue. This time, though, we aren't watching George the doorman. And we don't care about the elevator man. Because we have a new plan.

Raymond calls it Plan Y. He had outlined it in his notebook the first day we cased the building, then decided it was too risky. But considering Fats's desperate plight, no plan is too risky. And anyway, I like risky undertakings. They keep me on my toes.

The plan is this. Raymond has observed that a

great many deliveries are made to this building—from department stores, butcher shops, florists, fish markets, grocery stores, a jewelry shop called Tiffany. Surely there will be a delivery for Dr. Henry Simpson, Apartment 9F. Using the techniques I have perfected for bus travel, we'll be able to get not only inside the building but inside the apartment as well.

There is only one thing wrong with Plan Y, as I see it. We don't know for sure that Fats is inside the apartment. Perhaps by now he has been taken to the hospital, to those terrible cages. After a lengthy discussion, however, we have decided that the apartment is the place to start. It has been only three days. If Fats has remembered all I have taught him, he may have managed to escape detection by the deadly doctor. There may yet be time to snatch him back. If he is not there, we will have to come up with a new plan, one a lot more complicated than Plan Y.

Raymond checks his pocket watch.

"Ten o'clock. The deliveries should be starting any time now," he predicts confidently. "Watch for small trucks with store names on the sides. Or bicycles. Butcher shops and fish markets usually deliver by bicycle. And drugstores deliver on foot. We need to spot each delivery as it approaches, so we'll be ready to go into action."

"Right," I agree.

Raymond takes the left side and I take the right, surveying our surroundings for deliveries.

The street is quiet, like no one gets up early in this part of town. There aren't even any limousines parked out front. A few taxis cruise by, a bus, but no small trucks with store names on the sides. I turn my attention to the sidewalk.

A man in a gray suit is walking briskly toward us. I look him over carefully. But all he is carrying is a briefcase. This is not a delivery.

A couple of minutes later a baby carriage, pushed by a woman in white nurse's shoes, approaches. This is not a delivery. Then I spot another set of wheels—bicycle wheels. This appears more promising. I lean out to take a closer look, and discover that the bike is being ridden by a little kid. This is definitely not a delivery.

"Watch out, Marvin!"

Instantly, like the well-trained athlete that I am, I

dive back into the bush. And not a second too soon. *Sniff-snuffle-snort.* Some sort of animal is investigating our hedge.

"What is it?" I whisper.

"Dog," Raymond whispers back.

Snuffle-wuffle. Snort-snort. It sounds more like a lion or tiger to me. Then a wet black nose appears, just inches from my own. And wrinkly brown skin.

And long floppy ears. It's a bloodhound, just like in the movies.

Raymond and I press back as far as we can, against the rough stone of the building. I can feel Raymond trembling. My own knees seem suddenly a little weak.

Grrrrrr-uff! The nose twitches. The lip curls, revealing a set of regulation-size white fangs.

I take a deep breath. Raymond looks like he is going to pass out.

"Peaches, what is the matter with you?" asks a woman's voice. "Come out of there this minute."

Grumble-mumble. Sniff-snort. Very slowly and reluctantly the nose retreats. And with a final *snuffle* it is gone.

"Whew!" I wipe the perspiration from my brow. "That was a close one."

Raymond sinks into a heap on the ground. He is shaking too much to speak.

I am the first to pull myself together. "The deliveries!" I remind Raymond. "We may have missed some."

Once more we take our places. And immediately I spot something. A pair of legs, standing on the sidewalk in front of me. The legs are dressed in dark-blue trousers. They could belong to a delivery man.

This time I check carefully for dogs before leaning out to take a closer look. There is something familiar about these blue legs, but I can't quite put my finger on it. As I follow the legs upward, to the blue jacket with gold buttons, the blue hat, the nightstick, it becomes more and more familiar. This is no delivery man. It is a cop.

I poke Raymond. "Look at this," I whisper.

He looks. Then he pinches me. "Look at *this*."

At the curb is a small truck. But instead of a store name on the side, it has the initials N.Y.P.D. New York Police Department. The door opens and three more cops get out.

"Oh, no!" I hiss in Raymond's ear. "They're on to us. We've got to get out of here!"

Raymond looks at me strangely.

"On to us? But, Marvin, we haven't done anything wrong."

I stop to think about it. I'm so used to running from the cops that I've forgotten that this time we are innocent. We are only trying to save Fats's life.

It makes me a little nervous to be so close to my old enemies, but I stand my ground and wait to see what they are up to. At first glance it seems odd. All four cops go around to the back of the truck and start unloading some long wooden things. They set them up on the sidewalk. I recognize the long wooden things right away. They are police barricades, the kind of barriers the cops use when they want to keep people away from a hole in the street or the scene of a crime. But what are they doing here?

I can't figure it out. I glance at Raymond. He looks puzzled too. But then I hear him say, "Ah, of course. What else could it be?"

I give him a questioning look, and he whispers in my ear, "Remember what it said in the newspaper article? The animal lovers were going to demonstrate today against cruelty to mice at the doctors' offices. They must have found out where Dr. Henry Simpson lived and decided to demonstrate here too. And the police were called in to make sure the protest is peaceful."

I nod. Of course. What else could it be?

And sure enough, just as the cops finish setting up the barricades at the curb, a crowd begins to gather. Just a few people at first, mostly women and children, and so far I don't see any signs. But probably they'll be arriving any minute now. I could write a few signs myself, like: "Doctors Who Torture Mice Are Bad Medicine," and "Mice Are Nice," and "Free Fats and the Skinny 500."

More and more people are gathering, and it is obvious that no deliveries will get through to 999 Fifth Avenue this morning. Raymond looks worried and keeps mumbling, "We've got to get inside. There must be a way." But I am smiling. Never before did I realize that New York was so full of mouse lovers.

The cops are having trouble keeping people behind the barricades. And we are having trouble seeing what is going on, with so many people milling around on the sidewalk. All we can see from our observation post is shoes and shopping bags and stroller wheels. I still can't see any signs.

All of a sudden there is a murmur in the crowd. "They're coming," someone says, pointing up the street, and the word spreads. "They're coming. He says they're coming." It must be the signs.

With that thought, I can contain myself no longer. I can't stay hidden in a hedge when I could be demonstrating for all mousekind. As the crowd presses forward against the barricades, I step out into the open.

"Marvin, what are you doing?" cries Raymond. "Have you gone mad?"

"I have to see this," I tell him. "Courage, Raymond the Rat. These mouse lovers won't harm us."

He doesn't look convinced, so I grab him firmly by the ear and move forward. Between legs and under strollers and around bicycle wheels we go until we reach the barricades. It is easy for us to slip underneath. Now we are in the front row. Now we can see what everyone is looking at.

We hear it before we can see it. Drums. *Rat-a-tat-tat. Boom, boom.* And then cymbals. *Clang, clang, clang.* And then, suddenly, a whole brass band dressed in bright gold uniforms marches into view. And following the band is a line of girls in short skirts twirling batons, and then a bunch of men on horseback, and then another marching band. I can't believe my eyes. "What a demonstration!" I yell at Raymond through a blare of trombones.

Raymond is frowning and yelling something back. But I can't hear him because now the tubas are passing by. He points to a sign on the front of a float. It reads: "St. Andrew's School Salutes Greek-American Day."

I don't get it. And then the tubas are past, and I can finally hear Raymond. "It's not a demonstration," he is shouting. "It's a parade!"

A parade! Of course. Fifth Avenue is famous for its parades. I feel a momentary twinge of disappointment that all of this is not in honor of us. After all, if there is a parade for Greek-Americans, why can't there be one for mice? But I can't stay downhearted for long, not with the flags and the floats, the music and marching. I love a parade.

So it is that by the time the third marching band comes strutting by, my tapping toes will remain still no longer.

"Come on, Raymond!" I cry.

"But—Fats. Our rescue mission," he protests.

"Later," I say.

90

And grabbing Raymond by the ear, I get out there where I belong—between the cymbals and the bass drum and just behind a high-stepping drum majorette, marching in the Greek-American Day parade down Fifth Avenue.

9

I Go Inside

"Good morning, Marvin."

I open my eyes, and for a moment I don't know where I am. What is all this green stuff that surrounds me? What is this strange sweet smell in the air?

And then it all comes back to me—our glorious march in the Greek-American Day parade from 81st Street all the way to 70th Street, where we were forced to drop out due to Raymond's aching feet. Our decision to camp out in Central Park overnight, brought on by Raymond's insistence that he could not possibly take another step. And then the nightmare that was last night.

Camping out is cold. And it's hard on the bones, especially when you are used to a nice soft doll-house bed with a quilt to pull up around your ears. Not only that, but there is all this empty space around you—space filled with dark shadows and strange rustlings and squeaks that could be a dog or an owl. I hardly slept a wink. This must be what it is like to live in the country. I'll take the city any day.

I sit up and stretch and take a deep breath. "Ah-ah-ah-choo!" Now I see what the sweet smell is coming from. We have been camping out in a bed of crocuses. Yuck. I prefer the pungent aroma of sub-way platforms and back alleys and overflowing garbage cans.

Garbage cans remind me that I am hungry. We didn't have a thing to eat all day yesterday except for a bit of stale hot dog roll that we found under a park bench. I look around me for food. But all I see is grass and flowers and trees.

"What do mice eat in the country, anyway?" I ask Raymond.

Raymond scratches his head. "Seeds, I believe," he says. "And berries. Things like that."

"Seeds? Berries?" This is ridiculous. I've got to get back to civilization. "Come on, Raymond," I order. "Let's go find a garbage can."

It takes a few minutes, but finally I sniff one out, next to a children's playground. It's nice and full. Our breakfast consists of part of a strawberry ice-cream cone (the cone part), a pretzel, two animal crackers, half a chocolate-chip cookie, and a few drops of orange soda. It's not caviar, but I've had worse. As we are brushing the crumbs off our whiskers, Raymond sighs. "If only Fats were here. This is his kind of breakfast."

Fats! I'd forgotten all about Fats with the excitement of the parade, the terrors of our camp-out, and then my empty stomach. Fats is still waiting to be rescued. Every moment lost brings him closer to disaster at the hands of the deadly doctor. And here we are eating chocolate-chip cookies.

"Raymond!" I say, leaping to my feet. "Have you forgotten? We have a job to do. If we are successful, Fats will have his next breakfast with us."

So we march back up Fifth Avenue. It's not as

94

much fun without the brass bands and the floats and the costumes, but we make it to 999 Fifth Avenue before noon. The building seems back to normal. No cops, no barricades, and George the doorman is just finishing sweeping up the candy wrappers and broken balloons littering the sidewalk. We take our places once more inside the hedge.

"There should be extra deliveries today," Raymond points out. "To make up for yesterday."

And sure enough, we've only been there a few minutes when a boy rides up on a bicycle. "Delivery for Freeman, Four G," he tells George the doorman. The doorman presses a button and speaks into the intercom. "A package from Harvey's Fish Market, Mrs. Freeman." Then he tells the boy, "You can take it right up."

A minute later a blue truck with the name "Sunshine Florist" printed on the side pulls up next to the awning. A man gets out carrying a long white box. "Delivery for Keating, Ten B." Again George the doorman speaks into the intercom. And again he sends the delivery man upstairs.

"See what I mean?" whispers Raymond.

I see. Plan Y looks promising. In fact, I can tell

it's going to be a snap. All we have to do now is wait.

We wait. And wait. There are deliveries from the drugstore and the dry cleaner and the delicatessen. There are deliveries from Saks Fifth Avenue and F.A.O. Schwarz and Macy's. A fur coat is delivered. And a seven-piece dining room set. More flowers. And a gigantic stuffed pink rabbit.

But none of it is for Dr. Henry Simpson, Apartment 9F.

"I can't believe it," Raymond mumbles morosely as a man from United Parcel unloads six dress boxes from Bergdorf Goodman for Freeman, 4G. "That's her fourth delivery. And still nothing for Nine F."

I sit down again. All this jumping up and down whenever a truck appears is starting to get to me. I'm worn out from doing nothing.

"What time is it?" I ask Raymond.

He consults his pocket watch. "Four fifty-two," he reports. "It's getting late for deliveries."

I check the sidewalk to the left and to the right. I check the curb in front. Nothing seems to be coming. I pace up and down on what is now a well-worn path inside the hedge. Is it possible that the deliveries for the day are finished? Forty-seven packages and not a single one for Dr. Henry Simpson. It's unheard of. It's a disgrace.

Raymond is slumped against his knapsack, the picture of dejection. Gazing up through the leaves in the general direction of Apartment 9F, he whispers, "Fats, wherever you are, we're sorry. We tried."

I follow his gaze. I don't know which windows are 9F, but somehow in my mind's eye I can see them. They are covered with heavy iron bars, and behind the bars are drawn shades. As I look up, a new and terrible image drifts into my mind. Inside the darkened room are cages, row after row of them. It is the doctor's home laboratory. And inside one of those cages, lying limp on the floor, is Fats. I can see him now, not the Fats we used to know, but a new Fats. A Fats without fat, licking listlessly at the bars of his cage while he dreams of a peanut butter and watermelon-pickle sandwich. He was never a fussy eater, but not even Fats can make a meal out of steel. A Fats without hope. A Fats without friends.

No! That part at least isn't true. "Hang on, Fats," I mutter grimly. "We're still trying."

Just as I say these words, I catch a fleeting

glimpse of bicycle wheels rolling past, turning in, stopping. And a voice says, "Groceries for Simpson, Nine F."

Am I hearing things? Can it be true?

"Raymond!" I hiss.

He scrambles to his feet. Peering through the hedge, we see a boy standing next to a bicycle with an enormous basket. And in the basket are two boxes of groceries.

George the doorman is speaking into the intercom.

"Get ready to move," I warn Raymond, bouncing eagerly on my toes.

The doorman says, "All right, you can go up. Take the service elevator."

With that I'm off like a shot. The boy lifts one box out of the bicycle basket and sets it down on the floor. As he turns to get the other one, I make a flying leap—up and over the side of the box. I hear Raymond right behind me. But for once he doesn't land on top of me. I slide down a milk carton, carom off a loaf of bread, and sink into something cold and damp and slippery. It folds itself around me. I am trapped in its embrace. For a moment I almost

panic. But then I notice a familiar smell. It reminds me of the greenery of Central Park. I take a small nibble. Yuck—lettuce!

I've never been fond of vegetables. But there is only one way to escape the clutches of a head of lettuce. Bite by bite, I eat my way out.

"Raymond," I whisper.

"Over here" comes the reply.

Raymond is stretched out on top of a bag of miniature marshmallows, his cheeks stuffed, his whiskers sticky. "Now, this is the way to travel," he tells me. He reaches through a slit in the bag and pops another marshmallow into his mouth. "Care for one?"

I shake my head. I'm too full of lettuce. But I join him for a soft ride.

We are in the elevator now. I hear feet shuffling, cables clanking. The floor beneath us lifts, and up, up, up we soar. Then abruptly we lurch to a stop. There is more foot shuffling, and our grocery box is suddenly lifted. I feel myself falling off our soft marshmallow bed onto something that feels very much like the prickly top of a pineapple.

But I don't care. For as I fall, I hear the delivery

boy say, "Groceries for Simpson." And a woman's voice replies, "Bring them right in."

We've made it. We are inside Apartment 9F at last.

10

I Make the
Acquaintance of Emily

Plunk! The groceries are set down again. And the woman's voice says, "Wait here while I get my change purse."

There is not a second to lose. We have to get out of this box before she starts unpacking the groceries.

We climb out of the pineapple ("Ouch, that stings," complains Raymond), up the loaf of bread and the carton of milk, and peer over the top of the box. The woman is nowhere to be seen, and the delivery boy is looking the other way.

"The coast is clear," I hiss at Raymond. But not

too clear. I can hear the woman's footsteps already returning.

We just have time to drop down onto a blue tile counter, to notice that we are in a large, sunny, yellow-painted kitchen, and to dart behind the nearest large object—a round ceramic jar—before she is back again.

"There you are," she says to the delivery boy, and we hear the jingle of change.

"Thank you," says the boy.

We hear the back door close. We are alone with the woman in the kitchen.

We settle ourselves into the small space behind the jar. It's cramped and not nearly as comfortable as sitting on a bag of marshmallows, but it seems safe. And it may be a good place to observe what is going on in the apartment of Dr. Henry Simpson.

It turns out to be an excellent observation post. We can't see anything, because it is too risky to poke our noses out from behind the jar, but we can hear everything.

The woman, we soon learn, is the cook. We can tell this because she talks to herself as she bustles around the kitchen, unpacking the groceries, putting them into cupboards, opening and closing the refrigerator, rattling pans.

"Only three for dinner again tonight," she mumbles, stirring something on the stove. "Going to the theater, Mrs. Simpson says. Meeting the doctor for dinner first."

The doctor. A chill passes over me as she says the words. We are in the right apartment, that's for certain.

"I don't know why they even bother to have a cook," the woman goes on. "Never eat at home. Never give me a chance to prepare my special sauces. Plain meat and potatoes, that's all Mrs. Cleary cares about. And Emily—that child doesn't eat enough to keep a bird alive."

Mrs. Cleary. Emily. Who are they? Raymond and I look at each other questioningly. Then it comes to me in a flash of brilliance that I know part of the answer. Emily is a child. The Dolly-Deluxe doll carriage was purchased for a child. So, I deduce, Emily must be the child of Dr. Henry Simpson. It's elementary. But Mrs. Cleary—we'll have to wait and find out who she is.

We don't have to wait long. Just as interesting

aromas begin to waft around the kitchen ("Mmm, blueberry muffins," I observe. "Tapioca pudding," sighs Raymond.), a door opens and someone comes into the kitchen. Two people. I know immediately who they are.

"Emily, there you are. How was school? And your ballet class? Supper will be ready in five minutes, Mrs. Cleary. You can sit down at the table and I'll dish it right up."

The cook chatters on, but I don't hear Emily or Mrs. Cleary saying anything. I can't help myself. I have to see for myself what these two look like.

Cautiously I inch my way around the jar.

"Don't do it, Marvin. Come back!" whispers Raymond frantically. But I keep going, farther and farther, until I reach a point where I can see all three of them.

The cook, a red-haired, red-faced woman in a white uniform, is standing at the stove, spooning something onto three plates. At the table sits a little girl, maybe six or seven, with long straight brown hair. She's not smiling or talking. Her face looks sad. This must be Emily. And next to her sits a stout, starched-looking woman also dressed in a white uni-

105

form and also not smiling or talking. She can only be Mrs. Cleary. As soon as I glimpse the uniform, I know what she is. It's a strange thing. Children who live in other parts of the city are taken care of by their mothers. But children who live on Fifth Avenue are taken care of by nurses in white uniforms. I can't figure it out, but that's the way it's done. Mrs. Cleary is Emily's nurse.

I feel something tugging at my tail.

"Okay, Raymond, okay," I grumble, and I retreat behind the jar. I've seen what I wanted to see. Now I can go back to listening.

For a few minutes there are only the sounds of eating. Then the cook starts talking again.

"Did you meet any nice playmates today, Emily?"

At first there is no reply. Then a small, soft voice says "No."

"You must realize, Mrs. Scott, that Emily moved here only six weeks ago. It takes time to make new friends." That is Mrs. Cleary. Her voice is as starched as her uniform.

Silence again, except for forks clicking.

Then that tiny voice asks, "Where are my mother and father tonight?"

"It's the theater tonight," answers the cook. "And the benefit concert tomorrow night. And your father has an early appointment in the morning. So he won't be here for breakfast."

Again a pause. And then Emily says, "He's never here." Her voice is as sad as her face.

Raymond and I exchange looks. Of course, Dr. Simpson is never here. He's over at the hospital, torturing mice.

107

"Emily, you've hardly touched your chicken pot pie. Come now, take a few bites. I've made your favorite dessert."

And a minute later, "Are you sure you won't have thirds, Mrs. Cleary?"

"Oh, thank you, Mrs. Scott, but I couldn't."

We hear dishes being cleared from the table. And the cook's footsteps going to the refrigerator to get the dessert.

"Here you are, Emily. Tapioca pudding—your favorite. Would you like an oatmeal cookie to go with it?"

"Yes, please," says the small voice.

This time the cook's footsteps come in our direction. In fact they seem to be coming straight at us. *Clomp, clomp, CLOMP.*

"Marvin!" squeaks Raymond in alarm.

There is no time to do anything. Nowhere to run, nowhere to hide.

"Shrink" is all I can tell Raymond.

We crouch down. We try to make ourselves invisible. But it's no use. We can't crawl under the jar.

CLUMP. The footsteps stop right next to us.

Raymond has his eyes closed, but mine are wide

open. I want to look death right in the eye before it takes me.

And so I catch a glimpse of red hair and a red face just before a giant hand, also red, descends upon us. Closer and closer it comes. Larger and larger it gets.

It's all over, I know it now. My final thought, before that hand grabs us, is: We should never have hidden behind a cookie jar.

11

I Lead a Midnight Raid

"Do you mean to say I'm still alive?"

Raymond says it like he can't believe it. His eyes are open now, but he still looks dazed.

"You only fainted," I reassure him.

"But," Raymond persists, "the footsteps, the hand."

I nod. "When I saw that hand, I thought it was curtains for sure," I admit. Closer and closer, larger and larger. And then, at the last possible second, the hand lifted the lid of the cookie jar and reached inside. And we escaped undetected.

After I explain all this to Raymond, he manages to sit up. "That was too close for comfort," he says. "In the future we will have to choose our hiding places more carefully."

Now that Raymond's collapse is over, I turn my ears once more to the kitchen. Things have quieted down, I notice. Emily and Mrs. Cleary have departed, and there are only the soft sounds of water running and silverware clinking as the cook cleans up.

I don't dare peek out after our recent narrow escape. But I don't need to. In a few minutes I can hear her talking to herself again.

"Well, that's it then. Everything spick-and-span. I'll just put the leftover pudding in front where the doctor can see it, in case he has a mind for a midnight snack."

The refrigerator opens and closes one more time. And then, one by one, the lights go out. A door closes. And we are alone.

For several minutes I don't move. She may have forgotten something. She may be right back. But when the kitchen remains silent and dark, I get to my feet.

"It may be a trick," warns Raymond.

But I don't think so. After all, nobody knows we are here.

I slip around the side of the cookie jar until I get a full view of the kitchen. It is, as the cook said, spick-and-span. Everything has been put away neatly for the night. The only light comes from a crack under the door leading to the rest of the apartment, and from one dim bulb that burns over the stove. That's in case the doctor has a mind for a midnight snack, I figure.

The thought makes me shiver. What if the midnight snack he has a mind for is a cookie? We had better, as Raymond said, choose our hiding places more carefully.

I edge back behind the jar.

"The coast is clear," I inform Raymond. "Now, here is the plan."

First we are going to switch hiding places, from the cookie jar to a group of three other jars I can see at the end of the counter. "Sugar," says one. "Flour," says another. "Rice," says the third. No one is going to make a midnight snack out of any of these. We will stay put there until the doctor and his wife come home, turn out the lights, and go to bed. This could be late. Midnight, or even later. Then we are going to venture forth and look for Fats.

"An excellent plan," Raymond says approvingly. "Bold, yet cautious."

It takes only a moment to scurry from the cookie jar to the one labeled "Sugar." We slip behind it. Immediately I know we've made a good choice. It's darker here. And roomier. I feel safe. So safe, in fact, that after a few minutes I begin to yawn.

"What time is it?" I ask Raymond.

He checks the clock above the stove. "Seven thirty."

"Wake me up at midnight," I order.

I am deep in slumber when I feel something shaking me. "Go away," I mumble. "It's not morning yet."

"It's midnight," whispers Raymond.

Instantly I am wide-awake. This is the moment I have been waiting for. And I am ready for action.

"Have you seen or heard anything?" I ask.

Raymond nods. "At exactly eleven twenty-six," he reports, "the front door opened. I heard voices, a man's and a woman's. I couldn't quite make out what they were saying, but I feel certain it was the doctor and his wife. Then the voices faded away. At precisely eleven thirty-nine the light under the door went out. Since then it has been completely quiet."

Eleven thirty-nine. That was twenty minutes ago. Enough time for the doctor and his wife to have gone to bed. But what if he went to bed and then decided he had a mind for a midnight snack?

"We'll wait twenty more minutes," I decide. "To be on the safe side."

At twelve twenty everything is still dark and silent.

"Now," I tell Raymond.

Stealthily we creep out from behind the sugar jar. We look over the kitchen once more in case there is something we missed, like maybe a cat or a burglar alarm. Nothing. We descend from the counter to the floor, then dart across to the door that leads to the rest of the apartment. Here we pause a moment, catching our breath, listening for sounds on the other side. Again, nothing.

Now I step back to survey the door. Doors are a nuisance when you are our size. They tend to have locks or they're made out of steel or—most inconvenient of all—they revolve. I have yet to encounter a door I couldn't penetrate, using my mighty muscles or my crafty brain, but it can take time. And tonight we are running out of time.

Looking more closely, I see that this door doesn't have a lock or even a doorknob. It's a swinging type. They are usually heavy. This will require a wedge, or perhaps a battering ram. Then I notice something that makes me breathe easier. There is a large crack underneath. We won't have to go through the door after all. We can go under it.

I point out the crack to Raymond. He nods. We each take a deep breath, then squeeze under. It's lucky Fats isn't with us. We just make it.

We find ourselves in the dining room. And what a dining room it is. There is a long polished oval table, surrounded by enough chairs to serve a banquet, and over it hangs a crystal chandelier that gleams, even in the darkness. There are gold drapes and gold candlesticks and gold-framed mirrors. And the walls are covered with paintings in heavy carved frames. I blink. This is not what I expected at all. Where are the barred windows and the cages?

Of course, I tell myself. They wouldn't keep the

cages in the dining room. We have to search the rest of the apartment.

I nudge Raymond, who is looking at the paintings with his mouth open. We proceed to the next room.

The next room is not really a room, but a foyer filled with bookshelves and more paintings. And the front door. I make a mental note of its location for future reference.

Directly ahead is another huge room. I can tell at a glance that this is the living room. There are some velvet couches with carved backs, a marble fireplace, a grandfather clock, and still more paintings.

"It's like a museum," whispers Raymond, gazing in awe from the doorway.

"Keep moving," I growl. I know we will find no cages in the living room.

We turn down a hallway, which is lit by a tiny flower-shaped light in the ceiling. My heartbeat quickens. I sense that we are getting closer. If Fats is here, we will soon find him.

"What's that?" Raymond clutches at my sleeve.

I listen. From a room at the end of the hall comes a faint but distinct sound. A kind of rhythmic moaning. *Wheeze-sigh. Wheeze-sigh.* Is it Fats? Is it five hundred mice crying for help? No. Suddenly I know exactly what it is. It is the doctor—or maybe his wife—snoring.

So now we know where the doctor's bedroom is. I decide to investigate that room last. First we will check the rest of the doors on this hallway.

There are three of them. The first is a bathroom, an ordinary elegant bathroom with brass faucets and a shell-shaped sink. Could there be anything hidden behind the green-and-gold-striped shower curtain? Boldly I push it aside. All that is behind it is a shower.

The next door looks more promising. It is slightly ajar, and I can see the edge of something that looks like shelves. This could be it. The doctor's home office. His laboratory. His torture chamber. I tiptoe up to the door. I listen. It's very quiet inside. But then, his victims would probably be too weak to squeak.

"Come on," I hiss at Raymond. He has become distracted, staring up at the paintings in the hall.

He joins me. For a moment I hesitate, afraid of what we may find in this silence. But then I think of Fats and I step into the room.

Shelves. That's all I see at first. They line one whole wall. But on them are not cages of mice, but shoe boxes. Row after row of shoe boxes and, farther down, sweater boxes and shirt boxes. On the opposite wall is one long metal bar, from which dresses and coats and skirts are hung. There must be a hundred dresses here. It looks like the Better Dresses department at Macy's. This is not the doctor's laboratory, but his wife's clothes closet.

I back out of there fast. As I do, there is a terrific *bong* overhead, followed by a deeper *boom* from the living room.

Raymond leaps into my arms. "They're on to us!" he squeals.

My first thought is that we've tripped a burglar alarm. But then I hear, from some far corner of the apartment, a faint *cuckoo*.

"Don't be ridiculous," I snap at Raymond. "It's just the clocks striking."

Raymond gets down. "Sorry, Marvin," he says contritely. "My nerves are on edge."

We continue down the hall, to the third door. This one is also slightly ajar. I have only to glance inside and I know immediately whose room this is.

A pink night-light illuminates a scene that reminds me of a Macy's display window at Christmas. There is a four-poster bed, complete with lace canopy and piles of pillows and a ruffled pink bedspread. There are matching curtains at the windows, a tall white bureau, a little round table and chairs. But what really makes us blink and look at each other in disbelief are the toys. If the doctor's wife's closet was like Better Dresses, Emily's room is like the toy department. There are toys everywhere—stuffed animals, a wooden rocking horse, shelves filled with books and games, a giant blackboard, a three-story dollhouse. And then there are the dolls—baby dolls, boy dolls, girl dolls, rag dolls, old-fashioned dolls with china faces, dolls from other countries. Never before, even in Macy's, have I seen so many dolls in one room. And, of course, there are doll beds and doll high chairs and doll strollers.

Raymond suddenly gives me a sharp elbow. He points to something that is almost hidden in the shadows in a corner near a window.

I can hardly believe my eyes. It is the Dolly-Deluxe model doll carriage.

We have tracked it down at last. I, Merciless

Marvin, master detective, have triumphed again. But have we also tracked down Fats? It's not possible that he is still inside. Or is it? We have to take a closer look.

Now is not the time to do anything rash. I study the room long and carefully. Nothing stirs. I check the four-poster bed. It is so high, so piled with ruffles and pillows, that I can barely make out the tiny figure lying there like a princess in a fairy tale. But I see long dark hair spread out on a pillow. I see an arm curled around a teddy bear. Emily is fast asleep.

Beckoning Raymond to follow, I step into the room. We stick to the shadows close to the wall. From the door to the bureau we scamper, under a chair and behind the bookcase. We emerge near the window. And finally we are there, standing next to the Dolly-Deluxe doll carriage.

Again we pause to look and listen. And again everything is still.

"This is it," I whisper in Raymond's ear.

I step up on a wheel, grab a metal spring, and pull myself up on it. Then I reach down to give Raymond a hand. Together we inch our way up the metal frame, get a leg over the top of the carriage, and peer inside.

Something is sleeping there, covered with a woolly pink blanket.

"Fats?" I whisper.

There is no answer.

I look more closely. The something is wearing a dress and has a china face. It is a fat, curly-haired baby doll.

I look at Raymond. Raymond looks at me.

"Poor Fats," he sniffs.

I nod. Suddenly I know with an awful certainty that we will never see Fats again.

"What's that?" Raymond clutches at my sleeve.

I listen. It's a tiny sound, barely a sound at all, but it seems familiar somehow. *Wheeze-sigh. Wheeze-sigh.*

I look over at the bed. The sound is not coming from there, but from somewhere closer by. Like maybe the old-fashioned wicker baby basket that is next to the Dolly-Deluxe doll carriage.

Signaling Raymond to follow, I slide down the frame of the carriage, then leap to the floor. In sec-

onds I've scaled the baby basket and am standing in the folds of a pink satin ribbon that encircles it.

I listen again. *Wheeze-sigh.* There is no doubt about it. The sound is coming from inside the basket.

Cautiously I poke my head up until I can see inside.

The sight that greets my eyes is not to be believed. The basket is filled with pillows—lace pillows, eyelet pillows, satin pillows, velvet pillows. Sprawled out in the middle of this pile of pillows, looking fatter than ever, wearing a pink ribbon around his neck and a smile on his sleeping face, is Fats.

12

I Take Up Residence on Fifth Avenue

"Fats, is it really you?" asks Raymond in a bewildered voice.

I, too, can hardly believe my eyes. This is not exactly the Fats we expected to find.

I lean over and pinch Fats, to see if we are dreaming.

His eyes flutter open. The smile on his face broadens. "Hi, guys," he greets us.

After everything we have gone through to get here, the dangers we have dared, the obstacles overcome, this is all he has to say to us?

124

Perhaps he thinks he is dreaming.

"It's all right, Fats," I reassure him. "It's really us, and we're here to rescue you. But we've got to move fast, while everyone is still asleep."

Fats blinks. He is awake now, all right, but he looks puzzled. "Rescue me? Move fast? But why?"

Is it possible that he doesn't know what is going on here—the doctor, the cages, the cruelty to mice? Or could it be that his fat, contented condition is the result of some diabolical new medical experiment?

"Why?" I repeat. "Because you are living in a den of iniquity, that's why."

And Raymond and I proceed to recite to him all the horrors described in the newspaper story about Dr. William Frost and Dr. Henry Simpson.

"Oh, dear," clucks Fats. "Tsk, tsk." But he makes no move to flee. The only move he makes is to fluff up a pink satin pillow. "There must be some mistake, Marvin," he says calmly.

"What mistake?" I demand. "This is the apartment of Dr. Henry Simpson, isn't it?"

"That is his name," admits Fats. He carefully arranges the satin pillow, then sinks back against it.

"But you see," he says slowly, "Emily's father is a dentist."

We both stare at him in disbelief.

"A dentist?"

"The kind who fixes teeth?"

"It can't be."

"It's a cover-up."

"On the other hand," Raymond says thoughtfully, pulling on his whiskers, "I suppose it is possible. In a city as large as New York there could be two doctors with the same name. Especially as ordinary a name as Simpson."

"He *is* a dentist," insists Fats. "Really he is. Look at this."

He pushes aside a lace-trimmed pillow near his head. Behind it is an absolute treasure trove of candy: two lollipops, three foil-wrapped chocolates, a roll of Life Savers, several gumdrops, a Snickers bar, and a stick of licorice.

"Lollipops are my favorites," confesses Fats. "Emily gives me all the candy she gets from the elevator man and the lady at the dry-cleaning store. Her father won't let her eat sweets on account of they're bad for her teeth."

"You mean . . ." I am incredulous now. "You are saying that Emily knows you are here? That she set you up in this—this den of luxury and she feeds you on chocolates and lollipops?"

Fats nods happily. "Not just chocolates and lollipops," he corrects me. "Sometimes she brings me a cookie or a marshmallow. And she talks to me and plays with me and holds me on her lap. I am her friend. So you see, Marvin, I don't need to be rescued. Thanks for stopping by, though. And now, if you'll excuse me . . ." He yawns, stretches, and closes his eyes.

I look at Raymond.

It is hard to believe that our rescue mission has come to this. To see a sinister situation change in an instant to one of sweetness and light. To be rejected by the victim we've risked our lives to save. It's not fair. It's not just. It's not the way it turns out in the movies.

"Well," says Raymond reluctantly, looking down at Fats. "If that's the way he wants it."

"Wait," I say suddenly. "Wait just one minute." After coming all this way, I am not about to take no for an answer. I am not about to stand idly by while I lose half my gang. Still, I can't rescue someone who is kicking and screaming. My agile brain clicks into action.

"Fats." I nudge him with my foot.

His eyes open. "What is it now?" he asks grumpily.

"I was just wondering," I say casually. "Who besides Emily knows you are here?"

"Oh, nobody," answers Fats. "I am a secret." His eyes close again.

"Aha!" I snap. "Just as I thought. And do you know why you're a secret? I'll tell you why. Because it is a well-known, sad-but-true fact that no one welcomes a mouse in his house. Emily's father may be just a dentist, but he is dangerous just the same. And so is his wife, and the cook, and that Mrs. Cleary. If any one of them were to discover you, you'd be tossed right out with the garbage—or worse."

"Worse," puts in Raymond grimly. "Much worse."

"You guys worry too much," Fats protests. But his eyes are wide open now. "I'm all right. Emily will take care of me."

"A mouse can never worry too much," mutters Raymond.

"And how can Emily take care of you?" I ask. "Doesn't she go to school every day?"

"Well, that's true," admits Fats. "But while she's gone, I hide under the pillows. Like this." He burrows beneath a pile of pillows until all of him but the last half inch of his tail disappears. "See?" he calls in a muffled voice. "I'm perfectly safe."

"Your tail is showing," I inform him.

"A mouse is never perfectly safe," intones Raymond mournfully.

"Fats, old boy," I say, "what do you think would happen to you if someone decided to wash all these pillows?"

"Or give Emily's room a spring cleaning?" adds Raymond.

"What if her mother decides Emily's room is too full of junk?"

"Or that she's too old for dolls?"

"How about if they go on vacation? These Fifth Avenue people do it all the time. They might fly off to Miami."

"Or the South Seas. Or around the world."

"They might not come back for weeks."

"Or months."

"They might *never* come back."

Fats's nose resurfaces. And then the rest of him. "Never?" he says.

I nod. "It's been known to happen."

Fats sighs. "Okay, okay," he mumbles. "I give up. You can rescue me."

"Oh, good," says Raymond, his worry lines disappearing.

"You've made the right decision, Fats, old boy," I assure him.

Raymond is rummaging around inside his knapsack. In a moment he comes up with a small, bent, used-looking green object. He brushes it off on his sleeves.

"Here," he says, presenting it to Fats.

For a moment Fats just stares. He sniffs. He begins to drool. "A pickle," he whispers, his eyes as big as gumdrops. "Lollipops are tasty, of course, but a pickle!" He takes a bite, and suddenly goes into that ridiculous dance he always used to do when he smelled cheese.

"Same old Fats," Raymond says, smiling.

And then, in the midst of his jubilation, his stomach bobbing and pickle juice running down his chin, Fats falters. His step slows and his eyes cloud. Abruptly he stops dancing.

"What is it?" Raymond and I ask in unison.

"It's Emily," he replies. "Oh, how can I leave her, even for pickles? She needs me so."

I'll tie him up, I decide, and take him out of here kicking and screaming.

"What do you mean, she needs you so?" inquires Raymond.

"I am her only friend," says Fats. He collapses on the pillows, his pickle in one hand, a lollipop in the other. I can tell he is upset. When he is upset, he eats nonstop.

"Poor Emily," he says softly. He takes a lick of the pickle, then a lick of the lollipop. And he goes on to explain why Emily is poor.

It is a story we already have an inkling of, from eavesdropping on the cook in the kitchen. Emily is new to the city. She moved here in February, from California, where there is no winter. Her mother and father are busy. The other children at school already have friends. She is shy and lonely. But when Fats tells it, the story becomes even sadder. Here is Emily, a girl who has everything, a whole toy department in her room. And yet she has nothing because she has no friends.

"Poor Emily," says Raymond, shaking his head sadly. He puts a paw on my shoulder. "Everyone needs a friend."

But I hardly hear him, for once again my brain is racing. We can solve Emily's problem, and get Fats back where he belongs. I know we can. There is nothing to it.

"Fats, old boy," I announce, pulling up a light blue velvet pillow and making myself comfortable, "move over. We are joining you."

Fats looks startled.

Raymond looks confused.

"Just for a little while," I tell them. "You say that Emily needs a friend? Well, we are going to find her a friend."

13

I Create a Commotion

So we move in.

I'm not made for the lollipop-and-pillow life—and besides, we don't know how Emily would like having three pets instead of one. So Raymond and I look around for another residence.

My eye immediately falls on the three-story dollhouse.

"She never plays with it," Fats assures me.

That settles it. Raymond and I make ourselves comfortable at our new Fifth Avenue address. This dollhouse makes the one at Macy's look like a bungalow. It's so big that we each have not only a room of our own but an entire floor. And the furnishings are as elegant as those in the doctor's apartment. There are velvet couches, a chandelier, a grandfather clock, even tiny paintings on the walls. I don't feel as at home here as I do in our Macy's house. You have to keep your tail tucked in so you don't break anything. But for a temporary residence it will do.

And, like the dollhouse at Macy's, it provides us with a good view of what is going on. Within two days we know everything that is happening in Emily's life.

Which isn't very much. At seven o'clock she gets up, has breakfast, plays with Fats for a few minutes, and then gets ready for school. At exactly eight fifteen Mrs. Cleary calls her to go downstairs and wait for the school bus. She gives Fats a kiss on the nose, and is gone. She is gone until three fifteen. When she comes home, she goes first to the kitchen for a snack and then to her room. At about three forty-five, pushing the Dolly-Deluxe doll carriage with the fat baby doll inside and Fats concealed under the doll blanket, she goes for a walk in Central Park with Mrs. Cleary. After that it's supper in the kitchen with Mrs. Cleary and the cook, play with Fats for a few more minutes, and then bedtime. In two days we catch sight of Emily's mother only once, when she stops to say good night on her way to the ballet, and we don't see her father at all.

"Where is he?" asks Raymond.

"Out," says Fats.

This time I picture him at his office torturing patients with a drill.

Emily's schedule does not allow much opportunity for finding a friend. She is either at school or under the watchful eye of Mrs. Cleary. As I see it, there are only two possibilities: We accompany her to school or to Central Park. Going to school with Emily would be fun, but maybe a little tricky. I'm not sure my gang is up to it.

"I think the park is the best bet," I tell them.

It is the morning of the third day. Emily has just left for school. Before she went, she dressed Fats in a doll's fuzzy white sweater and hat. He looks like a marshmallow. But he doesn't seem to care. "If it makes Emily happy, it makes me happy," he explains sweetly. Yuck. All this sweetness and light is making me sick to my stomach. We've got to get Fats out of here before he turns into a marshmallow.

"The park," I repeat. "What do you think of it? As a place to find a friend, I mean?"

Fats pops a gumdrop into his mouth. "There are a lot of children there," he volunteers. "I can't see them when I'm under the doll blanket, but I can hear them."

Raymond nods in agreement. "I observed hundreds of them the day of the parade—children on bicycles, children on roller skates, children playing tag, playing ball, playing jump rope. But"—a frown of worry wrinkles his forehead—"how is Emily going to meet them?"

"That," I inform him, "is child's play. We will perform the introductions. Now, here is my plan."

It is three seventeen P.M. Raymond and I are concealed beneath the fat baby doll's eyelet pillow in the Dolly-Deluxe doll carriage. This is not the ideal way to travel. We are suffocated and squashed. But we are safe.

"Come on, Emily," I mutter to myself. "Let's get this show on the road."

Minutes go slowly by. Then I hear light, quick footsteps approaching, footsteps I have come to recognize as Emily's. "It's about time," I grumble.

I hear books dropped, the closet door open and close. And then Emily's footsteps coming closer, stopping next to the doll basket. "Hello, Chester," she says in her soft voice. "Did you miss me while I was gone? Look what I brought you. A whole peanut butter cup." *Chester?* What a dumb name. Doesn't she know she's dealing with a member of the toughest mouse gang in New York?

After a few more minutes of this, I hear her say, "Are you ready for your walk, Chester?"

I reach over and tweak Raymond's ear. "This is it," I whisper. It is the only risky part of my plan.

The carriage quivers as Emily arranges Fats and covers him with the doll blanket. She doesn't touch the pillow, though. "There," she says. "Now you're nice and cozy."

And then the carriage is rolling. Even though I can't see a thing, I can sense where we are. Out in the hallway waiting for the elevator, then going down, with Mrs. Cleary discussing with the elevator man the fact that it is almost spring. Then through

138

the lobby, past the unsuspecting doorman, and onto Fifth Avenue. As I feel the change in temperature, I can't help myself. I have to come up for a breath of cool, refreshing, sooty city air. This is where I belong—not cooped up in a fancy dollhouse in a fancy Fifth Avenue apartment, but on the streets of New York.

I duck back under the pillow before Raymond can get panicky. The carriage rolls along, up and down curbs, waiting for red lights. And then I can sense that we are in Central Park. The traffic sounds are farther away, and I can smell the greenery. Up a hill and down we go, the carriage slows, and I hear Mrs. Cleary's voice say, "We'll sit here today, Emily."

The carriage stops. There is some rustling as Emily and Mrs. Cleary sit down. And then silence.

I am tempted to come up for another breath of air and a look around, but I restrain myself. This is not the time. Instead I listen. And I can hear them— children running and laughing and shouting to each other. "Come on, Andrea!" "Wyatt, wait for me!" Soon, I tell myself, they'll be calling, "Come on, Emily!"

"And how are you today, Emily?" asks a voice. But it isn't a child's voice. It sounds like Mrs. Cleary, but with a little less starch.

"Fine, thank you," says Emily's small voice.

"Won't you join us, Mrs. McBride?" invites Mrs. Cleary.

"Well, now, I don't mind if I do," answers the voice. "I almost didn't come today. Gerald has a bit of a sniffle. But it is such a beautiful day, and I do think fresh air is important. So I just put an extra blanket in the carriage."

She and Mrs. Cleary go on and on about spring colds and teething and diaper rash. It soon becomes clear that Mrs. McBride is another nurse and that Gerald, who is only a baby, is not a likely candidate to become Emily's friend.

The two nurses are so busy talking that I realize that this is our chance. Now is the time to have a look around.

I tweak Raymond's ear to get him moving, then slip under the blanket to alert Fats. The three of us burrow our way to the foot of the carriage and, with the blanket still over us as a disguise, peer out.

The first thing I see is blue sky. And bright sunshine and trees just starting to leaf out a delicate light green. Mrs. McBride is right. It is a beautiful day. The next thing I notice is where we are. The bench overlooks a large pond. Children are sailing boats on the pond, and roller-skating and bicycling around it. It is the perfect spot for executing my plan. And then I look at Emily. She is sitting on the bench reading a book, a sad look on her face.

I can't stand it another minute. I am going to see to it that she runs and laughs and shouts like the other children. Right now.

The nurses are busy talking, Gerald is busy sleeping, Emily is busy being sad. I give Raymond and Fats each an elbow. We throw off the blanket, and silently drop down the side of the carriage.

We land in a heap in a clump of tall grass. We can't stay here, so close to the bench. I spot a large tree root nearby. "Come on," I hiss. Fats doesn't budge. He isn't used to such exertion. Probably he hasn't moved out of a reclining position since he met Emily.

Raymond and I drag him to his feet, and shove him behind the root. He promptly collapses, huffing and puffing. I can see that he is going to require total rehabilitation before he is fit to rejoin my gang. "Rest," I tell him.

I poke up my head to see where we are. As it happens, we are in precisely the right strategic location. Next to our tree is a path leading to the boat pond. A lot of children come down this path. One of them is about to be introduced to Emily.

"The marbles, please," I order.

Raymond digs into his knapsack and comes up with our emergency escape kit. I pass out the marbles, two to each.

"Your ammunition," I say. "When I give the signal, let them fly."

"Right," says Raymond.

"Check," says Fats.

I am the lookout. I keep watch on the path. In a moment I detect the approach of wheels. It is a stroller. A father is pushing it, and in it is a small boy. I look him over. Too young, I decide.

A couple of minutes later two girls come dancing down the path to the music of a portable radio. Too old, I tell myself.

And then I spot her. She looks about Emily's age, and has long blond hair and patent leather shoes.

Best of all, she is pushing a doll carriage. She is perfect.

"Ready." I poke Fats to make sure he is awake.

"Aim." I line up my marbles carefully.

"Fire!"

We let loose our marbles, right in front of the girl's feet.

We are right on target. The girl stumbles, her arms waving wildly in the air. And then her patent leather shoes slip out from under her. She falls.

My plan is working perfectly. Now Emily will come over to help the girl, and soon they will be pushing doll carriages together.

But there is an unexpected development. As the girl falls, she lets go of the doll carriage. It continues down the path without her. Now it crosses in front of a boy on a skateboard. He falls. A boy on a bicycle and a girl on roller skates are coming down the path. They swerve to avoid the fallen bodies, and go out of control.

"Look out below!" shouts the boy. He runs right through a large bush, narrowly misses a black poodle, and lands in the pond.

Somehow the poodle lands on the skateboard, which also hits the water, followed by the doll carriage and the girl on skates.

"Mommy!" she cries.

Mothers come running. Nurses come running. Everyone is shouting or crying or barking. A policeman comes roaring up on a motorcycle. It is a scene of complete pandemonium.

I Create a Commotion

We watch in fascination the chaos we have caused. Then suddenly I remember the reason for it all. Emily.

I look over at the bench. Emily is on her feet. She looks as if she wants to come over to help the blond girl, who is still sitting in the middle of the path. But Mrs. Cleary has her by the arm.

"My, my," she says in disgust. "Such a commotion. Come, Emily. We are going home."

14

I Fly High

"Never in my life have I seen such a commotion," says Raymond, shaking his head.

It is later that night, and we are sprawled out on pillows in the doll basket, munching on M&M's and reviewing the events of the day.

"It was pretty spectacular," I agree modestly.

"The crashes!" sighs Fats. "The splashes! That old lady diving into the pond to rescue her poodle!" He smiles at the thought. His stomach begins to vibrate. It bobs. It heaves. And then he is rolling around on the pillows, howling with laughter.

Raymond and I are forced to sit on him.

"Sssssh," I warn. "You'll wake up Emily."

"Emily." Abruptly Fats's laughter subsides. "We didn't find Emily a friend," he laments.

"It was a foolproof plan," I say. "But there were —uh—unexpected developments."

Raymond nods. He is twirling his whiskers thoughtfully. After a moment's reflection he says, "As I see it, the problem was not with the plan, but with its execution. Perhaps what is needed is a less violent way of attracting the victim's attention."

"Exactly," I reply. "Just what I had in mind."

Suddenly my spirits rise. I toss a pawful of M&M's in the air and catch them in my mouth.

"We'll try again," I tell my gang. "Tomorrow."

But we do not try again tomorrow. Because the next day it rains. Instead of going to the park Mrs. Cleary takes Emily and the Dolly-Deluxe doll carriage to the Metropolitan Museum.

"What was it like?" Raymond asks eagerly when Fats returns.

"Just a lot of coats and umbrellas," says Fats glumly.

Raymond looks puzzled.

"They checked me in the coat room," Fats explains. "Doll carriages aren't allowed in the museum."

And the day after that it rains again. Mrs. Cleary takes Emily to the ballet. Emily can't take the Dolly-Deluxe doll carrriage there either. But she takes Fats in her coat pocket.

"What was it like?" Raymond asks eagerly when Fats returns.

"Just a lot of loud music and people jumping around," Fats replies. "And they were wearing these funny outfits called tutus."

"Yes?" says Raymond. "And then?"

"And then it was so warm in Emily's pocket that I fell asleep," Fats confesses sheepishly.

The next day is Sunday. A sunny spring Sunday. I can see from the dollhouse window that it is a perfect day for a walk in the park. Not only that, but the park will be overflowing with children. Everyone goes for a walk in Central Park on a sunny spring Sunday.

"This is the day we find Emily a friend," I announce to Raymond.

We go to tell Fats.

But a strange sight greets our eyes in the doll basket. Sprawled out on a heart-shaped pillow, chewing disconsolately on a Tootsie Roll, is a roly-poly ballerina.

"Fats, is that you?" I ask.

"In a tutu?" Raymond echoes.

Fats nods glumly. "If it makes Emily happy," he says in a small voice, "it makes me happy."

Once again Raymond and I stash ourselves away under the fat baby doll's pillow in the doll carriage. Soon Emily returns from breakfast. We can hear her trying to teach Fats to pirouette. This is a sight I long to see with my own eyes, but Raymond keeps holding me down by the tail. At last we hear Mrs. Cleary's voice. "Emily, it's time for our walk."

A few minutes later we are rolling down Fifth Avenue. It is just as I thought. Everyone is out for a stroll on this sunny spring Sunday. I can hear them all around us. "This is the day," I repeat to the rhythm of the carriage wheels, "we find Emily a friend."

It is such a nice day that Mrs. Cleary and Emily keep walking. Into the park and uphill and down, and then uphill and down again. I am beginning to think they will never sit down, when finally I hear

Mrs. Cleary say, "Here is an empty bench, Emily."

As soon as they settle themselves on the bench, I surface. Right away I can see that we are in a different part of the park. Instead of a pond and lots of trees and paths, there is open space—flat green grass stretching as far as my eye can see. If it weren't for the city skyline in the distance, I would think we were in some vast green country meadow.

There are children here, too, of course. Some are running across the field, chasing balls, chasing dogs, chasing each other. "Too violent," I tell myself, remembering Raymond's words. Others are strolling quietly with mothers and fathers, dressed up in their Sunday best. "Too well guarded," I decide. Then I see something that looks more promising. A short distance away a group of girls are playing jump rope. Not too violent. Not too well guarded. And I'm sure Emily would like to jump rope.

I point out the girls to Raymond. He nods. All we have to do is devise a way of getting these jump ropers over to meet Emily.

We bail out of the carriage and dart behind a rock. Then we creep silently through the grass like hunters on an African plain. We are about halfway to the jump rope game when suddenly, in the grass right in front of us, there looms a large red object.

"Hit the dust," I hiss over my shoulder.

Fats collapses with a loud "Oof."

I flash him a warning look.

"I can't help it," he whines. "Have you ever tried to hit the dust in a tutu?"

I study the red object. It doesn't move. Cautiously I raise my head. The object is diamond shaped, and is constructed out of paper and sticks with a string attached to one end. The other end has a long knotted tail. It looks vaguely familiar. Can it be some sort of trap? Then I realize where I've seen it before: in Macy's toy department. It is a kite.

I have always been interested in flying objects. And I've never been this near to one before. I decide to take a closer look.

"But, Marvin," protests Raymond. "The jump rope game. What if they get tired and go home?"

"This will only take a moment," I tell him.

I walk all around the kite, investigate its tail, then slip underneath to see how it is put together.

"Be careful, Marvin," warns Raymond. "That thing could take off."

"Sure," I scoff. If only it were true.

I reach above my head and grab the place where the two sticks cross. I pretend I am soaring through the air, far above Central Park, riding high on a fresh spring breeze.

The kite seems to move.

It must be my imagination.

It isn't my imagination. My feet have left the ground. And I catch a glimpse of Raymond's and Fats's startled faces.

"Marvin, come back!" they cry in panic.

I hold on tight.

The kite lifts—an inch above the grass, a foot. And then, abruptly, it falls. I hit the ground, skinning my stomach, scratching my tail. I grit my teeth, but I don't let go. Nobody said flying was going to be easy.

The kite lurches upward again. A foot, two feet. And then I can feel it catch that fresh spring breeze. It rises gently, steadily into the air.

Looking down, I can barely make out Raymond and Fats. Though I can't see their faces, I know they are looking up at me with their mouths wide open. I see the jump ropers. And Mrs. Cleary and

Emily sitting on their bench. And a boy running across the field holding on to a string that goes up into the air. With a start I realize that he is flying my kite. Then, surprisingly, I am looking at the tops of trees. The pond is a puddle, buildings look like toy building blocks. And then I am up so high that all I can make out is a blur of green below.

I stop looking down. Who cares what is below? This is my great moment. I, Merciless Marvin the Magnificent, am flying at last.

It is as I always dreamed it would be. Cut loose from Earth, I float close to the clouds. The city below is a toy city, its dangers softened by distance. I soar above it in the sunlight, alone except for a single bird as daring as I. I am free. I am strong. I own this town.

I seem to be climbing higher. Perhaps I will climb above the clouds. I want to keep going, to see what is beyond them.

The breeze is stronger now. It gusts, making my ride a bit precarious. The kite zigzags. It sinks a little, then rises again. And then, without warning, it starts to fall.

Down, down, down I go. At any moment another

gust of wind will lift me. I'm sure of it. I cling to the crossed sticks and wait. But the kite continues to plummet downward.

Now I can make out the tops of the trees. The puddle becomes a pond again. The blocks are buildings. I see benches, bushes, bicycles. And the boy running across the field, taking in string, trying desperately to keep my kite aloft.

The trees are rushing toward me. It occurs to me that if I crash into one of them, it is all over. My great moment will have been my last. Closer and closer they come. I seem to be heading for a giant oak. I can make out its branches, then its twigs, then its budding leaves.

I close my eyes. Then I remember I always promised myself I would die with my eyes open. I force myself to open them again. And so I see the kite just brush the topmost branch of the oak tree, then plunge straight to earth.

Everything goes black.

Vaguely I hear voices. One sounds like Emily's. I struggle to open my eyes and see if it can be so.

Everything goes black again.

I am aware of more voices.

"Careful, don't move him. We must determine if any bones are broken." That has to be Raymond. And, "Here, Marvin. Have a lick of my lollipop. It will give you energy." That can only be Fats.

And then, for the third time, everything goes black.

15

I Bid Farewell to Emily

My eyes flicker open.

The world no longer looks black. Surprisingly it looks red.

It even smells red. Then I realize that I am looking at the world through a red lollipop.

I push it away. And there are Raymond and Fats, smiling at me.

"Congratulations, Marvin. You were magnificent."

"You did it! You did it!"

"It was rather an unusual way of attracting the victim's attention, but it worked."

"Have a lollipop! Have a jelly bean! Have something!"

I accept a black jelly bean, my favorite flavor. "Thank you, thank you," I say. "It was nothing really. All in a day's work. Uh—what exactly did I do?"

"Do?" cries Fats. "You found Emily a friend!"

They fill me in on all the details. It seems that my kite crash-landed in a bush not far from Emily's bench. She came over to see what had happened, and stayed to help the boy untangle the kite tail from the bush. So the voice I heard *was* Emily's. While I was lying unconscious under the bush, she and the boy were becoming friends.

"His name is Eric, and he goes to her school!" Fats tells me excitedly. "And guess what! Tomorrow after school she is going to his house to play."

It was a clever way of introducing them, I have to admit. Who else but I, Merciless Marvin the Magnificent, would have thought of it?

I reach for another jelly bean. As I do, I become

aware that I am no longer lying under the bush but in the cozy, cushioned comfort of the doll basket, a velvet pillow beneath my head, a soft pink doll blanket tucked around my body.

"But how did I get back here?" I ask.

"We carried you," explains Raymond. "It wasn't easy. You were out like a light. But Emily and Eric were so busy looking into the bush that they didn't notice what was happening under it. And Mrs. Cleary was reading her newspaper. We rigged up a sling out of string and our emergency handkerchief, and hoisted you into the carriage. After that, there was nothing to it." He looks me over, his forehead again creased with worry. "I don't think you have any broken bones. Just a slight concussion."

Gingerly I try out my various limbs. They are sore, but I think Raymond is right. Nothing is broken. My forehead, on the other hand, has a bump on it the size of a jelly bean. Slight concussion, indeed. I would call it a goose egg.

Still, considering everything, I feel good. Not everyone can fall out of the sky and live to tell the tale. Not only that, but it occurs to me that once again I have led my gang to glory. Single-handedly, against all odds, I have tracked down one mouse in a city of a million mice—a feat even more difficult than finding Santa Claus in Brooklyn. Along the way I have brought happiness to a poor little rich girl. And to top it off, I have done what no other mouse has done before me: I have soared close to the clouds. I am a hero.

I leap to my feet to take a bow.

My gang stares at me blankly.

"Well," I say, rubbing my paws together briskly. "That's that. Our rescue mission is complete. We have saved Fats. We have found Emily a friend. We can go now."

"Go?" says Fats.

"Go," I repeat. "Away from this lap of luxury. Back to back alleys and the last car on the subway and scrounging for a living. Back to the real world."

"Leave Emily so soon? Just when she's finally happy?" Fats looks shattered. "I want to see her smile. Just for a few days."

Raymond nods in agreement. "After seeing her sad so long, it would be nice to enjoy her happiness. Besides, we don't even know if she will stay happy.

What if she and Eric don't get along when she goes to his house to play? And thirdly, Marvin, what about you? Victims of concussion need plenty of bed rest. We should stay just a few days."

I have to admit that I'm feeling a little dizzy. I sink back against the pillows, and even allow Fats to cover me again with the pink doll blanket.

"All right," I tell them grudgingly. "But just a few days."

The days pass. My recovery is swift—naturally, since I am tough as nails. Soon I am up and about, knocking over furniture in the fancy dollhouse. My teeth ache from too many jelly beans. And I am beginning to have those restless itches and twitches in my toes. I know for sure it is time to move on.

There is no reason to stay. Emily continues to be happy. She goes to Eric's house to play. Eric comes to her house to play. They play in the park. She doesn't need Fats anymore. She has a friend.

When I mention this to Fats, he turns glum.

"Just a few days more," he pleads. "I love to watch her smile."

I can see what he means. It does even my tough

heart good to see Emily now. She smiles, she skips, she sings. She is a new Emily. But we can't sit around forever, watching someone smile. We have places to go, things to see, new adventures to seek.

I can see I am going to have to hit Fats at his weakest (though largest) point: his stomach.

"Fats, old boy," I begin, "it is true that it's nice to see Emily smile. But have you stopped to consider that her smile may be your downfall?"

Fats looks puzzled. So does Raymond.

"From my observation of Santa Claus," I continue, "I have noticed that one smile leads to another. Today Emily has a friend. Tomorrow she may have two friends, then three, then four. She will be playing with someone every single day after school. And then what will happen? I can see it all now. First she will forget to tuck you in at night. Then she will forget to bring you candy. And soon she will forget you completely. You will become sad. You will become hungry. You will become skinny." I glance ominously at his enormous stomach. It would take weeks without jelly beans before it would even begin to shrink. "You wouldn't want that to happen, would you, Fats?"

Fats looks anxiously down at his stomach. He pats it tenderly. "Well, no," he admits.

"Now," I go on, warming to my subject, "consider the alternative. If we return to the real world, we put spice back into our lives—action, danger, a few laughs. And"—I pause for emphasis—"variety into our diets. Tell me, Fats, when was the last time you tasted a salami sandwich? On rye. With maybe a slice of Swiss cheese. Mustard and lettuce. And a kosher dill pickle on the side."

"Swiss cheese," breathes Fats, his eyes glazing over. "Mustard and lettuce. And, did you say, a kosher dill pickle on the side?"

I nod.

He begins to salivate. He begins to tremble all over. And then he is on his feet, performing his famous cheese dance.

"Boys," I say. "We leave tomorrow."

It is another sunny spring day. Emily and Mrs. Cleary are on their way to the park. Emily is pushing the Dolly-Deluxe doll carriage, with the fat baby doll inside and Fats concealed beneath the doll blanket. Little does she know that Raymond and I are along for the ride too. And that this will be our farewell ride in the Dolly-Deluxe doll carriage.

Out the door of 999 Fifth Avenue we go.

"Good-bye, George," I mutter. "Keep the place neat and clean, old buddy."

Down Fifth Avenue we roll.

"Farewell, Fifth Avenue," I intone. "Your life is not for me."

Into Central Park we meander.

"So long, Central Park," I mumble. "Your life is not for me either."

Uphill and down we ride, and finally the carriage slows down. I hear Emily say, "I told Eric I would meet him at this bench, Mrs. Cleary. He's going to teach me to sail his new boat."

There is the sound of Mrs. Cleary settling in to read her newspaper. And then, a couple of minutes later, a voice calling, "Come on, Emily!"

"I'm coming!" Emily calls back. And I hear her racing lightly across the grass.

So. This is it. The moment for our departure. I give Raymond and Fats each a tail tweak and we go into action. Up from under the doll blanket, over the side of the carriage, and into the grass below.

We pick ourselves up and pause for a last look around.

We are standing at almost the exact spot where we caused the great commotion. I smile at the remembrance—boys on bikes, girls on skates, poodles on skateboards, all splashing into the pond. But now the scene is peaceful. Emily is sitting on the low wall that surrounds the boat pond. She is watching Eric launch a sailboat into the water. She is smiling.

"Let's move it," I order.

Fats hesitates. "But I didn't say good-bye to her," he whimpers.

"What good are good-byes?" I snap. "Let's go."

But Fats is suddenly bouncing up and down. "I've got it!" he cries. "I see it! The perfect good-bye for Emily. Just a minute, Marvin."

And without hesitation, or even any huffing and puffing, he darts over to the big tree root and comes back with something clutched in his paws. It is a dandelion.

"See? Isn't it perfect?" he babbles. "I'm going to put it on the doll pillow where she'll be sure to see it."

"Oh, all right," I say.

Raymond and I boost Fats back into the carriage, and seconds later help him down.

He lingers a moment more, gazing down the hill.

"Good-bye, Emily," he says softly, a catch in his voice.

"Good-bye, Emily," echoes Raymond.

"Good-bye, Emily," I add. "Keep smiling."

I gaze up the hill.

At the top I see a boy. He has something in his hand. It looks like a model airplane. He's about to launch it. If I were there, I might be able to stow away on board. Who knows? This time I might even soar above the clouds.

"Come on, gang," I order.

And I lead the way up the hill.